A
PASSING
SEASON

Richard Blessing

A
PASSING
SEASON

Little, Brown and Company
Boston Toronto

FIRST EDITION

The quotation on pages 166–167 is from "Directive" from *The
Poetry of Robert Frost* edited by Edward Connery Lathem.
Copyright 1947, © 1969 by Holt, Rinehart and Winston. Copyright
© by Lesley Frost Ballantine. Reprinted by permission of Holt,
Rinehart and Winston, Publishers.

Library of Congress Cataloging in Publication Data
    A passing season.
    Summary: Growing up in a town where football is
everything, Craig Warren tries to resolve his
growing ambivalence towards playing on the high
school team and making football the center of his
life.
    [1. Football—Fiction] I. Title.
PZ7.B6186Pas 1982   [Fic]   82–12740
ISBN 0–316—09957–0

BP

*Published simultaneously in Canada
by Little, Brown & Company (Canada) Limited*

PRINTED IN THE UNITED STATES OF AMERICA

For
Craig Blessing *and* Daniel Rapport
and for
all the old coaches:
Francis "Rock" Denning
Ed "Doc" Phillips
The Valley Swede, Ken Patrick
Don "Kid Speed" Jones

and for
Clair Bee
Most of all for Clair Bee

A
PASSING
SEASON

ONE

Autumn, Oiltown, Pa. Main Street, the men in khaki and their thin women. The Oiltown Hotel, a clothing store, the Army-Navy Surplus, McHenry's Drugs, two Kendall stations, a Gulf and a Penzoil, three five-and-dimes, the boarded-up windows of the places that went broke, the neon windows of the bars that didn't, one picture show. Above Main Street the houses, row on row of brown and gray and mustard yellow all darken to the color of wood smoke and refinery ash. And above the houses, high on the rutted hills, the trees turn dusky reds and oranges on their way to brown. The donkey pumps pound their clocklike tunes and the town keeps time. Or tries to.

Scrawny boys play touch football on every leaf-scattered lawn that's big enough, and their voices hang in the smoky air:

"I got ya right *here!*"

"This here's *two*-hand touch!"

"I *got* ya two hands!"

"You never!"

3

And little girls pretend themselves into cheerleaders on sidewalks where the hopscotch games of summer fade.

A tough town, a tough way to make a living. The men work grimly, dwarfed by the storage tanks, the derricks, the smokestacks. Until Friday night . . .

"Snowsuit weather," Craig Warren's mother would say. "Awwww."

"Bundle up. It'll be cold later," Mr. Warren would say.

The leaves would swish under their feet and they would walk through the dark toward the rattle of drums. They hurried toward the place where the sky was lit up. He had to reach up to take his father's hand. The grass was more green than storybook grass. The band was loud, like thunder, only more exciting. There were the smells of grownups. Coffee and cigars. Hotdogs.

There on those fall nights, all the khaki fathers lost their grimness and were excited kids again, and when the time was right, the crowd would begin to chant, "O–W–L–S, O–W–L–S, O–W–L–S," faster and faster until Craig Warren's heart was jumping in his throat. Then, when he couldn't stand it any longer, there they would be, the Oiltown Owls, exploding out of the dark tunnel under the stands and onto the unreal green of the field and the noise would grow until it stretched the black dome of sky above the hills. They were big and fast and easy in their grace and they wore black helmets and simple white jerseys with black numbers. The pants were white too, and without a stripe. Year after year, the plain black on white. It was a uniform for doing serious work on serious ground.

Across the way would be the blue of Brackenridge or the burnt orange of McKean or the maroon and gold of Oldfield. Sometimes it was the fancy green of City Prep. They were all too gaudy, Craig thought. A uniform should

4

say "No nonsense" and a team should be as simple and basic as the black-and-white Owls.

At the kickoff there would be a long rolling of drums and a shout like a gunshot. Then the white line and the bright-colored line of orange or blue or maroon would tangle and the players would swoop over the grass that was too green to be real, spilling one another with a terrible, reckless beauty. And all the proud fathers and their sons—along with more than a few of the mothers and most of the daughters—would shout and chant and sing and the cannon would boom after an Oiltown score and the band would play. Most of the time the big white line would drive the other back, their immaculate uniforms stained by grass and mud as the night wore on. By the fourth quarter the game was most often theirs, and some back would be racing through a hole and across the field and up and away along the sideline, or else a white jersey would drop back and the ball would soar in the night air and another Owl would be running free, behind everyone, and the ball dropping perfectly . . .

Back home, they would replay the game in the cramped living room. "Hit and spin," said Mr. Warren. "Hit and spin!"

"Look what you're doing to the rug," said Mrs. Warren.

Craig didn't care. He had a football that was stuffed with cloth. His father was on his knees, trying to keep him out of the end zone that was Mother's kitchen.

"Did I run good, Daddy? Did I?"

"Did I run *well*," Mrs. Warren said.

"We'll see how good you run when one of those big Oldfield tackles gets a crack at you. Then we'll see, bub. Now it's time for you to hit the hay."

"What a town," said Mrs. Warren. "No music, no

poetry, no theater. *Foot*ball!" She shivered. "Football is everything."

"Off to bed, bub. Off to bed," said Mr. Warren.

Saturday mornings the downtown quarterbacks met in front of the Oiltown Hotel. They hunched against the brisk winds in letter jackets of differing vintage and stages of disrepair. It was a kind of open house, men who had once played the game coming and going, stopping long enough to exchange insults and to compare the players of the night before with the heroes of other nights and other years. Joe Hugo was the unofficial president of the group, the oldest regular member and a kind of folk legend from his nights as a running back.

"How'd you like this kid Keller?" one of the men asked Joe Hugo.

"Good back," said Hugo, hitching his belt over his ample belly.

"Paper says he went over two hundred yards last night."

"That so?" said Hugo.

"Yup. Only nineteen carries it says."

"Good back," said Hugo, and spit carefully with the wind.

"Looks like some records might go down before Keller gets done," said another man. He was younger, still rangy and trim. "How many times did you go over two hundred, Joey H?"

"Enough," said Hugo.

"How many?" the younger man challenged.

"Seven," said Hugo. "Twice against Oldfield, twice against Brackenridge, once against Prep up there. Couple others."

"You shoulda seen him up to Prep," said another man.

"Three touchdowns over fifty yards and I ain't kiddin' ya. This Keller's maybe all right. He'll do. But Joe here . . ." His voice trailed off. Joe Hugo hitched his belt again and looked over the store tops to the hills and the bright-leaved trees.

Music and poetry and theater. Yes. And history too.

TWO

The sun was low over the grassy ski slope, throwing Craig Warren's long shadow in front of him on the stony and cleat-torn ground. The shadow distorted his neck, made the distance between the helmet and shoulder pads seem longer and more frail than it was. If you didn't look too closely, he was all football player. He was more than six feet tall and weighed about 175 pounds, most of it in the shoulders and chest, almost none of it in the waist and hips. But there was something wrong about the face, the expression in the blue eyes or playing over the mouth. "If I saw that look coming at me in a football suit," Coach Muldoon had once yelled at Craig, "I'd say, 'Boy oh boy, a picnic on the hoof!'"

"All right, ladies. Last play," growled Muldoon for the fifth time. It was late August, the tag-end of a long scrimmage during one of the last double practice sessions, and Muldoon wanted to quit on a good one. Craig scraped the ground nervously with his cleats, picked up a good-sized stone, and tossed it to the sideline. The rocks didn't bother Muldoon. What they cost in injuries, he said, they made up for in creating bad temper. Craig felt stiff, a little weak in the knees. He had spent most of the afternoon, a reserve quarterback, standing behind the first-team huddle while Clint Gold ran the offense. Now he was at defensive safety, and he watched uneasily as Gold looked up from the huddle, grinned thinly in his direction, and bobbed down again.

Craig watched them come out of the huddle with a clap and a roar. The Owls looked sharp. Willie White was the split end, at six feet five the tallest starter on offense. He could catch a basketball off the board in either hand and ram it through the hoop before coming down. Craig thought of White's speed and backed off a step. The tackles were both lettermen, Steve Bates and 260-pound Tiny Daugherty. Mark Thomas was at one guard, not as big as you'd like, but experienced and tough. The other guard spot was up for grabs, but Larry Bizarro had first shot at it and was looking good. Paul Pulaski was the center, a tough shift from being the star tight end of last year's jayvees, but the kid was almost mean enough to suit Coach Muldoon. Gold had been converted too, a 200-pound ex-fullback who doubled as a sprinter and a shotputter in the spring. "When you don't have a quarterback, you go with an athlete who can get the job done," was what Muldoon had told the newspaper when he made the switch. Gold didn't like it much, was only a fair thrower, but he ran the team well, was dangerous on the sprint-out, and handled all the kicking. The halfback was Johnny Zale. Already people were saying he would be another Joe Hugo or "Funny" Phelps or "Quick" Keller. The fullback was Jim DeSales, light for the job at 180 pounds, but a blocker who would clear some space for

Zale and Gold. Billy "Blitz" Krieg flanked to the right. Krieg had caught only six passes the year before, but four had been for touchdowns, and two had been game winners. The junior tight end was Eagle Duvall, and a coach at Penn State had said Eagle could start for them right then. He was six feet three inches tall and weighed a wedge-shaped 215. Muldoon liked him because he hit harder than anyone he had coached in twenty years. "Put all the ballplayers in the state in a dark alley," said Muldoon, "the Eagle is going to be the one to walk out. And he'll be smiling."

Gold bent to Pulaski. "Down. Brown thirty-eight. Brown thirty-eight. Hut—hut." At the snap Pulaski moved to his left and back, helping out Larry Bizarro, and Gold started his drop. From the corners of his eyes Craig watched Krieg and White start on deep routes and the linebackers began their drops into the hook zones. Three steps back, Gold planted his rear foot and started up the middle. Someone yelled, "Draw," but it was too late. The reserve linemen had been tempted into easy outside angles on their rushes, and Gold shot through and split the linebackers before they could react. That left only Craig Warren in his path. Gold was not a pretty runner. There was nothing effortless about the way his legs bunched and gathered or the way his free arm ripped at the air as he came. His cleats threw divots with every stride and his face contorted behind the mask of his helmet. Craig felt himself go to his knees and reach with his right arm, knowing he was doing everything wrong, knowing, too, that he was keeping away from those brutal knees. Then came a jolt that was almost like an electric shock and his arm went numb. The force of the blow spun Craig and dumped him to the ground as Gold charged on for another twenty yards before he slowed at the coach's whistle and circled back. Craig got up slowly, his face hot, while the Owls whooped it up. "All right, Goldy! All right, Big Gold!"

"Bring it in," yelled Muldoon, and they gathered around him. He was a short, wiry man with rimless glasses that he took off when he was angry, which was most of the time. They were off now. He ran a quick hand through tufts of hair that grew like steel wool at the sides of his head. Muldoon waited past quiet to absolute silence. The pumps in the hills clanked and rattled distantly and Craig could hear the players breathing. That was all. "Ladies," said Muldoon, "you don't help us by coming out here and letting us run over you. You don't help us by lying down for us. Warren, didn't the good Lord issue you some of the finest physical equipment that's out here? Didn't *we* issue you the best pads and equipment the taxpayers can buy?" Muldoon paused for effect. He made a sweeping gesture, taking in the whole squad. "Well, I'll tell you this: we can't supply backbone. You'll have to bring that one thing with you." Clint Gold made the mistake of snickering. Muldoon wheeled on him. "And you, Gold, you! 'Nice run, Goldy,'" he mimicked viciously. "Nice, my foot! Do you know how wide a football field is? You had the whole blasted field and you're *supposed* to be a sprinter and you decide there's no place to run but *over* the blasted safety man. Someday—by mistake—we'll have stuck a football player back there, Gold, and you'll try to run over him and he'll knock your hat off! And you know what? I'll stand over you and say, '*Nice* run, Gold-y!'" Muldoon put his glasses back on. "I dunno," he said. "I dunno. You should be getting a little mean by now. We've got Fort Steel in a week, and you know they'll send you home in a garbage bag if you don't get a little mean." He sighed. "All right. Ten forty-yard dashes up the ski slope and take it on in."

There was one drinking fountain in the locker room which, Muldoon said often, was one fountain too many. They lined up raggedly, sucking air, waiting their turns impatiently. When Craig bent to the water a sudden hand on the back of his head pushed his face in the flow. "Move it," said Clint Gold. "Let a football player drink." Craig moved aside as Gold shoved in. Suddenly Gold was against the wall, his cleats two inches off the floor. "Nobody," said Eagle Duvall, holding the husky quarterback without apparent strain, "*no-body* crowds in front of the Eagle when he's thirsty!" He smiled. "And the Eagle *is* thirsty." He turned to Craig. "I believe I was just behind you." He set Gold down. Craig drank hastily and Duvall turned his back on Clint Gold and let the water swish loudly around in his mouth.

Craig's face was hot. That was just like Duvall, Craig thought, some code out of a corny western—stand up to the gunslingers, protect the women and children.

"One of these days," Gold said, adjusting his jersey, "you're going to push it too far, Duvall."

Eagle spit the mouthful of water carefully over the quarterback's shoes. "You're the sprinter," he said. "You can most likely catch me." He walked away, not looking back. Clint Gold opened his mouth, thought, and closed it again. The line moved on, the jostling weary, but good-natured.

In the muggy green of the late summer twilight, a dozen kids were playing touch football on the nursing home lawn. A few patients and nurses sat fanning themselves on the mossy brick of the old porch. Craig Warren paused to watch. He was already late for supper and another minute or two wouldn't matter. Some of the kids wore white sweatshirts with black numbers spray-painted front and back. Well, they sure knew about the Owls' home uniform. What they didn't know about was the morning practice jersey that you wrung out at noon and pulled on again, still wet and cold, over the heavy pads still sopping with your own sweat and then wore to the afternoon session. Or about the ski slope. Or Coach Muldoon. One of the small players caught a pass niftily, taking it over his shoulder, and another raced over and tagged him lightly on the shoulder. And they didn't know about the driving knees of Clint Gold.

He went on past the familiar cramped houses, the small, dark paths between them strewn with abandoned toys, the people sitting on the porches or trimming the yellowing islands of their front yards. Dale Davis, who lived next door, was sitting on her front steps, reading. When she saw Craig coming she put her knees and toes together, clasped her hands in front of her, and fluttered her eyelashes. "Awwww. Gawrsh. Swoon. My football hero. Gawrsh. Swoon." They had started first grade together and she had been a chubby pal for nine years. In their sophomore year, last year, Dale had stopped being chubby. Her hair was short, a sun-bleached pixie cut, and it suited her. She had started to wear lipstick, pink, and Craig couldn't quite get used to the change. "Why don't you go have a few peanut butter sandwiches?" he said.

"Very funny," Dale said. "I—what happened to your *arm?*"

His forearm was raw and the blue of the bruise was already spreading. It hurt all the way to the shoulder. "I'm what's known as a 'bruising tackler,'" he said. "I

13

tackle 'em and I bruise. Maybe it'll keep me out of practice tomorrow." He had meant it to be light, but it came out all wrong.

Dale turned serious. "Why do you do it if you hate it so much?"

Craig pointed to the grass beside the steps. "Isn't that a snake?" He took advantage of her sputtering leap to retreat toward home.

"Craig Warren," she yelled after him, "if you ever have to eat the pigskin, it will be an act of cannibalism!"

He walked stiffly and painfully up his own steps, around the house to the back door. The old tire his father had brought home years ago still hung by a heavy rope from his mother's clothespole. All summer he had knelt thirty yards from that tire and, using just his wrist and forearm from one knee, he had whistled at least a hundred passes a day at and through the tire. Some days he had thrown more than three hundred times, and the grass between the place of his kneeling and the tire was worn to a memory. On washdays, of course, he had practiced elsewhere.

"I'll be *so* glad when school starts," said his mother, rattling the supper dishes as she put them on the table. "Then maybe we can regulate our lives again. This football until all hours of the night . . ."

Mr. Warren looked up from the sports page. "How'd it go, bub? And how long you going to let this fullback, this Gold, go pretending he's a quarterback?"

"So far he looks just fine, Dad, I guess," said Craig. "He'll be just fine."

THREE

The first week of school. Banners above the dim halls, above the trophy cases. *GO OWLS—BEAT STEELERS!* Dust particles rising in the slanting light of midafternoon. Beyond the many-paned windows the maples beginning to yellow. Sky of summer, wind of fall.

The students sat primly or sprawled lazily behind their scarred desks. Mr. Craft, the junior English teacher, new to Oiltown, only in his second year, stood with a hand on his plump hip in front of the blackboard. He was short and wore thick glasses and his soft hands often danced in little graceful pantomimes as he talked. No man's hands danced like that in Oiltown. No one else had a beard. The kids laughed at him behind his back and sometimes to his face. The year before, it was whispered, he had started to cry while reading a poem.

"Well then," Mr. Craft was saying in his soft voice, "why *does* Macomber tolerate such contemptuous behavior from his wife?" They were talking about a story called "The Short Happy Life of Francis Macomber." Craig had read it and liked it. It was about a man who was a coward,

15

then stopped being a coward and stood up to a buffalo charge. Then his wife shot him, maybe on purpose. It was hard to tell.

Dale Davis raised her hand. She was sitting by the window and the shadow of a leaf lay on her hair. "I think—sometimes—people just get used to seeing you one way for so long. They wouldn't see you any other way, even if you tried to change. Or even if you did change, they'd still see only what you were. Had been."

Mr. Craft nodded encouragingly. "Yes," he said. "Go on."

"That's all," Dale said. "After a while it just doesn't seem any use to even try. He's afraid that if he stops being afraid Mrs. Macomber will just make fun of him anyway."

Craig nodded. That sounded right. Dale would know. He looked around the room. Eagle Duvall and three other ballplayers were in the class. Three others, that is, if you counted Waldo Frampton. Frampton was a team joke. He wasn't big enough or fast enough or nearly agile enough, and worst of all, he was incurably good-natured. Nonetheless, Craig knew, Waldo Frampton was better off than Craig Warren. Frampton's lack of physical ability gave him an excuse. Nobody expected much from him. Meanwhile, he stuck it out, practice after practice, while the other players hid his football shoes or tied his practice jersey in knots or filled his helmet with shaving cream or liniment. He didn't seem to mind. And he never got in a game.

Craig was surprised to find his hand in the air.

"Yes, Craig. Have you anything to add to Dale's theory?"

"I think she's right," Craig said. "It's like if Macomber is afraid of the big thing—death—and he has always been afraid of it, same as most everybody is, then he's got to be scared of everything. His wife, other people, making mistakes. It's, well, it's consistent. But when—" Johnny Zale exploded with laughter, then covered it as best he could with a cough, whacking himself on the back and rolling his eyes apologetically at Mr. Craft. Frozen with horror, Craig looked at his hands. They were arrested in front of him where, a second or two before, they had begun to sway to the rhythm of the idea he had wanted to give a shape and a substance.

Mr. Craft ignored the interruption. He always left Zale alone. Craig wondered if the man were afraid. "Yes, go on," said Mr. Craft.

"There wasn't any more," said Craig, folding his arms, pinning his hands tightly beneath his biceps.

"You were in midsentence."

"I've forgotten," Craig mumbled. "Nothing important."

Mr. Craft looked disappointed. "How about you, Eagle?" he asked. "Can you help Craig out? Does what he was saying make sense to you?"

Eagle shifted his massive shoulders. His forearms all but covered the top of his desk. "No sir," he drawled, "it doesn't make sense. It doesn't make sense at all." He paused, then smiled reflectively. "Once though, when I was a kid, I had a buddy named 'Killer.' That is, he was named that till he got licked by a bigger kid on the Sixth Ward Playground. After that the bigger kid's skinny little brother used to push old Killer around like a baby buggy. Pretty soon everybody did it. Got so little girls could run him off the swings and merry-go-round. Seemed like if he couldn't whip everybody, he wouldn't whip anybody. By the end he got so little even the ducks were stepping on his head. We wound up calling him by his real name, which was Clarence." Eagle grinned. "So, no sir, it doesn't make sense, what Warren said about *consistent*. It doesn't make sense to the Eagle. But it happens. It sure does happen."

Mr. Craft smiled uncertainly. It was hard to tell whether Eagle Duvall was putting the whole world on with some enormous joke of his own or whether he was serious and hiding it behind lines about ducks stepping on heads. Maybe it was both. "The bell is about to ring," said Mr. Craft, and the students began closing notebooks and stacking them for the rush through the halls. "I did want to say, for those of you who will be absent tomorrow, those gentlemen who will be visiting Fort Steel, that we shall begin the poetry unit on Monday and that you are to read the introductory section in your texts for the occasion."

Zale groaned loudly.

"Needless to say," Mr. Craft added as the bell rang, "I wish our athletes godspeed."

In the hallway, Zale nudged Craig with an elbow. "Godspeed, Warren, old pip," he said, trying to imitate Mr. Craft and doing it badly.

"That's a lousy imitation," Craig said.

"You do a great one," said Zale. "In fact, I can't even tell you apart. Artsy-Craftsy, that's you. Hey, Eagle, whadya think? Which one's the real Artsy-Craftsy?"

"That one back there," said Duvall without interest. "This one here's missing a beard."

"Probably grow one if he could," said Zale, heading up the stairs to his locker.

"Zale's all right," Duvall said to Craig. "A good, tough kid." He grinned behind his cupped hand. "Not a whole lot bigger than one of those ducks, though."

Dale Davis was waiting at Craig's locker. "I could just

clobber you," she sputtered, and hit his locker with a tanned fist. "You—you—you jerk!" He was surprised, glanced back to see if Duvall were watching, but Eagle was busy in his next-door locker. "What did I do?" Craig wanted to know, fumbling with his locker combination, finally getting it. This was a Dale he had never seen before.

"Just because a—a *dope*—like Johnny Zale laughs, you quit. You didn't even try."

Craig made an effort to smile, but the muscles weren't working. "It's not a federal case," he said, his face reddening. "What's it to you?"

"Nothing," she said, "nothing at all. It's just that all you seem to care about is what you can't do—or won't do. Football. If you can't have that, you won't even do what you *can* do. You're *afraid* to be good at what you do best. Big star Johnny Zale might think it's *sissy* or something!" As if to punctuate her sentence, Dale kicked Craig's locker door shut with a hinge-rattling slam. Then she was off, almost running down the hall, dodging in and out of the clusters of students standing under the bright hand-lettered banners with giant cartoon Owls clutching mouse-sized Steelers in their talons.

Duvall leaned an elbow on Craig's shoulder. "Shame you and your girl can't trade tempers," Eagle said.

"She's not my girl."

"Worse yet," said Eagle. "Sounds to me like she has a good head." He watched thoughtfully as Dale swung around the corner and out of sight. "Rest of her ain't bad either."

Thursday evening the clan gathered. The downtown quarterbacks were out in force, shining up the front of the

19

Oiltown Hotel by leaning against it, watching the people straggling past, and talking football.

The question before the assembly was whether or not the Owls could handle Fort Steel on the Steelers' turf. "Surest thing you know," said Quick Keller, a worker now in the barrel house of the refinery. "Who else has receivers like White, Krieg and Duvall? Three best receivers in the state."

"Hell yes," said another ex-Owl. "Duvall's the three best receivers in the state all by himself. Ain't that right, Joey H?"

"Could be," said Joe Hugo, "only—"

"Could be?" exploded Keller. "*Could* be?"

"Last time I saw a game," Joe Hugo said, "fella couldn't catch a ball unless somebody threw one to him, and not up in the stands or on two hops."

"Gold can throw," said Quick Keller.

Hugo hitched his pants over a belly that had grown with the years. "Gold can throw a twelve-pound shot," he said.

"They're going to be thin," said a recent graduate. "Lot of them going both ways. And DeSales may not be the power runner you want." He brightened. "Johnny Zale," he said. "You wanna talk about runners, I've never seen his like."

"That so?" said Quick Keller.

"Runs good in the daytime," said Joe Hugo. "It counts under the lights."

Crowd roar. Trumpets and drums faintly from somewhere else, some other world. The Owls were stretched out on the floor of a locker room in Fort Steel, lying belly up on their black capes. Nobody said a word. From around a tile partition came the sound of retching. That was

Johnny Zale. Before Zale it had been Mark Thomas and before Thomas, Pulaski, the center starting his first varsity game.

Coach Muldoon strode up and down, stepping carefully over and around his players. His fist clenched and unclenched. "Be thinking about what you have to do," he said. "Be thinking about it." Silence. "Fort Steel is a good team, a mean, rough bunch. That's why we schedule 'em." Back and forth, the cleats clicking on the floor. "They won't throw thirty passes all season long, but they'll come at you with those horses, those big backs, and boys, you'd better be ready."

Craig Warren felt his body humming. He thought he might throw up himself. The hands clasped just under the big white 19 on his glossy black road jersey seemed to belong to someone else. They were hopelessly weak. He couldn't make a tight fist. He had one thing to worry about—holding for place kicks—and he wasn't sure his hands, those strange, large hands, would behave. It was odd to be staring at pipes on a ceiling in a room in Fort Steel, a room he would never see again and never forget. And it was odd to have somebody else's hands.

Muldoon had been in the room before. He'd won here and lost here and he knew it was a long ride home when you lost. "Rand and Strand," he said. "Strand and Rand. They may sound like a poem, but they're over two hundred pounds and they like to run." Silence again. "We've got to stick 'em, get 'em running with a little less abandon. Wachowiak is no quarterback. He's a guard who can count to five. If they want to throw—and they don't—they'll come in with Simon, number eleven." He was interrupted by a rush of noise from outside, a thunder of masculine voices, furious, almost hysterical in their rage, a booming of heavy fists against the door and the thin wall. That was Fort Steel, letting the Owls know they were there and on their way up to the crowd and the music and the lights.

Muldoon waited it out, smiling thinly. When it was quiet he said, "I'll tell you one thing. You back off from these people—you back off just one inch—and they'll run you all the way back to Oiltown. They'll run you home, they'll run you up your street and into your house and into your living room and they'll kick your behind until your nose bleeds. That's if you back off!" He whipped off his glasses, suddenly enraged by his own words. "But if I put any one of you—any man of you—in a circle with the man he's got to beat tonight, and if I said, 'Whip him, Eagle,' or Tiny or Goldy or Paul . . ." He paused. "Why, I believe that Fort Steel boy would get himself a whipping."

Muldoon put his glasses back on, picked up a cape. "Everybody up," he said. The Owls stood up, the pads bulging under the tight game jerseys. "Boys, I used to be a prizefighter. Some of you've been throwing up and a lot of you are feeling scared. Boys, I've been there. I did all that and more. But when I pulled on my trunks and left the dressing room, boys, I felt sorry for the poor sucker I was fighting." His voice dropped to a whisper. "Because, I'll tell you, I was on my way to murder him. And I'm feeling sorry—just a little sorry—for Fort Steel right now." And then he was shouting. "Because, boys, we are going to MURDER 'em!"

They went out then. Craig Warren had dropped his cape in front of the bench and was in the far end zone doing calisthenics before he felt his feet touch the grass.

FOUR

Sure hope none of those folks gets hurt over there,"
muttered Eagle Duvall. Craig looked across the field. The
Steelers were milling around their coach, and their
huddle was seething as they piled into one another with
uncontained readiness. The players on the outside leaped
on the stack trying to get some of the action, and the roar
of the crowd seemed to feed their excitement. They broke
out then to kick off, splendid in metallic gray helmets and
jerseys with numerals and stripes of scarlet. The Owls
were out, too, waiting, with Zale and Krieg in the deep
receiving spots. The drums began a gradually swelling roll
that seemed to go on forever. And then with a crash of the
bass drums the ball was in the air.

Zale took the ball two steps deep in the end zone, a
small black shirt getting larger in a hurry as he came
upfield and cut sharply toward the Owl bench. In their
eagerness, two Steelers overran him and another under-
estimated his speed and let him get to the sideline. Zale
was all the way to the 40 before they knocked him out of
bounds and onto the asphalt strip that served as the

runway for the long jump during track season. Craig was wide-eyed. They had growled like animals when they closed on Zale. "We'll break you, twenty-two! We'll break you!" one of them had snarled as he turned back to the field. Zale bounced up and headed for the huddle. Craig had to admire him. He could limp and swagger at the same time.

Zale tried a sweep, couldn't get to the corner, and the Steelers punished him again. Four of them were in on the tackle. On third down Gold dropped into the pocket. Krieg and White ran a crossing pattern and for a second Krieg opened up, but Gold threw to White and it was a tribute to the speed and leaping ability of the Owl split end that the pass wasn't intercepted. As it was, White had to go over a Steeler's back to slap the ball down. Fort Steel was ready to play.

Gold's kick was rushed, and Fort Steel took over just inside its own 30. There was nothing fancy about the Steelers. It was single-wing football except that Wachowiak handled the ball under the center before pitching to Strand or Rand and getting out in front to block. If he was nothing but a guard, as Muldoon had said, he was a good one, one who could not only head up the sweep but was agile enough to pitch back and lead off-tackle as well. The Steelers were double-teaming Duvall, sometimes with a guard and a lead back, sometimes with Wachowiak and Strand or Rand. And the rhyming backs did run hard, four, five and six yards at a crack, not much speed but a lot of power and determination. They moved that way to the Oiltown 23, first and ten, before Muldoon signaled for a time out. Duvall trotted to the sidelines and Wachowiak met with the Fort Steel coach across the field. Craig couldn't hear what was said, but Duvall nodded and trotted back, his helmet already streaked in places with the silvery paint of Steeler helmets.

Fort Steel came out of the huddle. Wachowiak barked the signals, pivoted and put the ball into Strand's stomach, and the big back followed Rand hard into the right tackle hole. The Owls closed down, the defensive backs coming up for the kill, before the bench saw it. Wachowiak had kept the ball, hiding it on his hip. "Pass!" But it was late, too late. Wachowiak couldn't throw much, but he didn't have to. His right end had blocked for a count, watched the Owl cornerback charge up, then slipped behind him into the open. He was all alone at the five, facing back toward the line of scrimmage when the pass wobbled into his hands. He held it over his head at arm's length, trotted into the end zone and almost contemptuously dropped it on the grass. Muldoon kicked the sawdust in front of the bench. "My fault! My fault! My fault!" Craig had never seen him so angry, the glasses off now almost continuously. Fort Steel kicked the point and came back upfield leading 7–0.

The kickoff sailed through the end zone. Even the Steelers' kicker was psyched tonight. Zale carried for a tough yard or two as the quarter ended. Craig was surprised. It didn't seem as if the game had any more than begun. Somewhere in the darkness of the stands behind him, his father was sitting alone. He had driven two hundred miles to Fort Steel, though Craig had warned him that he wasn't likely to play. "Long way to go to watch me hold for extra points," he had said. But his father came. Well, one quarter gone and he hadn't stepped on the bright green of the field. And he felt a deep and sudden shame as he realized he was glad he hadn't. For the first time in as long as he could remember, he didn't envy Johnny Zale. "No guts, no glory," Muldoon always said. Zale would earn his glory tonight. If he got any.

The teams battled on almost equal terms through the second quarter. Oiltown toughened up on defense. By the time Duvall and Daugherty had hit them a half-dozen times, they didn't run quite so hard. "Taking the brave out," was what Duvall called it, and neither Rand nor Strand was running with the abandon that had marked their opening series. It was a little like baseball, Craig thought. Any strong arm could fog it by good hitters for an inning or two. After that, only a real pitcher could survive. The problem was that the Owl offense couldn't get untracked. When the two-minute warning was given, they had only one first down, and that was with the help of an offside penalty that had set them up with a first and five situation.

They were stymied on their own 27. Gold dropped to pass, found everyone covered, and scrambled to his right. The linebacker in Eagle Duvall's hook zone reacted to stop the run, leaving Eagle momentarily free. Gold fired on the move and Duvall made a leaping grab at the 40. He was hit almost immediately, but he tore free and the crowd and the Steelers froze in horror. It was frightening to see Duvall moving at top speed in an open field. The safety played it cagey, giving ground, waiting for help, but Duvall didn't give him much room, barreling at him without making any attempt to fake or swerve. They finally ran him down, three of them, at the ten. He was at the three before they got him stopped.

The Owls called time then, called another one when DeSales and Zale came up a yard short after three cracks at the Steeler line. There were no time-outs left. Muldoon paced, polished his glasses, then barked, "Warren!"

26

"Yessir?"

"Go in for Krieg. Hold for the field goal. Tell Goldy to keep his head down."

He floated across the grass in a dream. His legs moved as if they were underwater, and his mouth was cottony. The huddle seemed miles away. He didn't think he'd reach it before the play began, and he half hoped he wouldn't. "Number nineteen, Warner, replacing number eighty-three, Krieg," said the tinny, disembodied voice of the public-address announcer from somewhere safe in the dark, playing games with names and numbers. And there were the Steelers, angry giants with grime and some blood on their scarlet and gray uniforms. "Fresh meat! Fresh meat!" "We gotta stick 'em! You hear me Kolo? Stick somebody!" "Hit! We win it here! HIT!"

"All right," said Gold to his line. "Lock it up. When you're ready, Pulaski." They came over the ball, each lineman placing his inside foot carefully around the ankle of the man next to him. If Fort Steel wanted to block this kick, they'd have to come from the outside to do it, and that was where Zale and DeSales were waiting. Craig knelt seven yards behind the ball, and Gold backed off his step and a half. "Show some guts," said Gold. "Give me a good hold."

Pulaski's snap was high and to the right; it tore through Craig's sweaty fingers like soap in a bathtub. Horror crawled in his stomach as he spun and raced after the ball which bounced and rolled back across the 20 and on toward midfield. Gold was out of it. He had kept his eyes riveted to the place where the ball was to be spotted, and all his momentum had taken him forward with his kicking motion. It was all up to Craig, and nothing seemed real to him as the din from the dark stands mingled with the snarl of the Fort Steel linemen as they gave chase. He picked

27

the ball up, lost it again. It felt waxy, ungrippable. Then he had it, he didn't know where—somewhere behind the Fort Steel 25, he knew that—and turned and saw them coming. They were not faces, but masks; not boys like himself, but monsters in nightmarish costumes. One of them got a hand on his thigh, spun him around, and then he was free of the hand but alone with four or five of the Steelers closing in.

Craig Warren then did the worst thing he could have done. He heaved the ball blindly in the direction of Clint Gold, heaved it and ducked as the silvery gray shirts slammed into him and drove him to the lime-striped grass. He guessed the worst even before they let him up, guessed it from the crowd noise and from the quick way in which one or two of the Steelers pushed away from him and started toward the Oiltown goal line. Zale was in pursuit, but it was too much to make up. A Steeler linebacker had stepped in front of Craig's gift toss and run through the lights and the cheering to an easy touchdown.

An enraged Eagle Duvall fairly threw the blocking back on his side into the ball on the try for point, leaving the score Fort Steel 13, Oiltown 0. And that was the half.

FIVE

The star after Clint Gold's name in the program meant that he was the team captain, but the Owls took their emotional life from Eagle Duvall. His fury was contagious, and they began the second half in the same murderous spirit with which he had ended the first. The kickoff unit left Steelers strewn on the field like gray leaves, pinned them back inside the 20, and came back to the bench seething at not having done better.

Craig Warren sat on the bench like a blind man, taking in through his ears and his nerve endings the speed and violence that surged back and forth in front of him. He had expected Muldoon to yell at him during the half. Nothing. He had expected rage from the other Owls, even punches. Nothing. Nothing. He pulled the black cloak closer around him and tried to forget.

Because if you could just forget, nothing came back, people, places, words. *We'll see how good,* his father had said, *we'll see how good you run when one of those big Oldfield tackles . . .*

Wachowiak's game plan had simplified. A two-touchdown lead meant that the Steelers had only to do what they did best—play ball-control football—to hold on and win. The problem was that the visiting Owls wouldn't cooperate. Wachowiak gave it to Rand. Duvall and Daugherty hit the big back high and low and left him getting up slowly with a yard loss. Wachowiak gave it to Strand going the other way and Pulaski and Mark Thomas rattled him with a hit that was heard in the top row of the stands. Another loss. The Steeler quarterback thought of a pass, thought of what his coach would have to say if anything went wrong, and gave it to Strand up the middle. He got two yards and bruises. Wachowiak wasn't worried. Not yet. Punt it. Get some field position. Wait it out.

No music, no poetry, no theater. Football is everything!

Strand had to hurry his kick, didn't get much height, and Zale took it with room to run at midfield. He flashed over the 40, cut at an almost ninety-degree angle to the right sideline, turned up again inside the 30, juked, stutter-stepped, reversed again, headed for the left sideline, got a block from Bates, a block from Pulaski, a block from—no. He was out of bounds at the Steeler 13 yard line. Muldoon was pacing again. "*One* more block! *One* more block!"

Look what you're doing to the rug!
Hit and spin, hit and spin!

DeSales cracked inside the 10 on first down. Gold rolled right behind some angry blockers on second down and the Steelers finally ganged up to bring him down somewhere inside the five. "Where is it? What's the yard line?" Muldoon was yelling at the field, but no one heard him. Zale hit the quick dive behind Bates and Thomas, and the referee waved the chain crew ahead. First and goal at the two. Zale hit it again and the Owls thought he had it—Willie White had his arms high signaling touchdown—but the officials spotted the ball just short. Gold held his palms inches apart, looking to the bench on his way to the huddle. Muldoon clenched a fist, jabbed it shortly in the direction of the end zone.

Boys, I've been there. I did all that and . . .

Gold took it himself on the sneak, climbing Pulaski and sliding back and lunging again, reaching with the ball. This time the officials had their arms in the air as the enraged Steelers drove the Owl captain back to the five and flung him to the ground. Touchdown!

I got you right here! You never!

Muldoon glanced his way. Craig Warren stared straight ahead. The coach had Billy Krieg by the arm. "Get back in and tell Goldy to go for two points with the sprint-out." Gold never looked for the pass, just tucked the ball under his arm and ran. He was lucky. When he went down the nose of the ball grazed the broad goal line, and the Fort Steel lead was cut to five at 13–8.

Wachowiak wasn't happy. Rand was going into his act, grimacing and sucking air and groaning a little to let the quarterback know it was someone else's turn to carry. And Strand, who was game enough, couldn't get untracked, especially since his running mate's blocking had lost its early enthusiasm. "C'mon Rand, you're dying on us," Wachowiak snarled, but it didn't do much good. The Owls dared him to throw now, shooting linebackers on almost every play, the cornerbacks creeping up and up until they started each play less than five yards from the line of scrimmage. From there they followed Wachowiak and plugged holes like linebackers and tormented the ballcarriers with punishing tackles. The stocky quarterback glanced at the clock. It barely moved. Punt and hang on. Punt and hang on.

When the quarter ended the score was still 13–8, but the Owls whooped it up as the teams changed ends of the field. "Fourth quarter! Up the slope now! Up the ski slope! Fourth quarter!" It was their ball on their own 34.

Ladies, Muldoon said, *you don't help us by lying down. . . .*

Gold overthrew Krieg, who had beaten the safety and was running free. On the next play the big quarterback began his drop, stopped short, and charged up the middle on the same quarterback draw that had left Craig Warren sprawled on the practice field a week earlier.

you don't help us by . . .

The safety, fooled badly a play earlier, had read the play as a pass all the way, and his retreat left Gold a huge seam to run in. He used his speed, veered to the sideline, and made the defensive backs take the long, ground-yielding angles to converge on him and knock him out of bounds at the Steeler 29. "All *right!*" howled Muldoon.

"Sometimes they listen," said Bill Buckwalter, the backfield coach.

If he couldn't whip everybody . . .

DeSales got nothing on a trap. Gold lost almost ten yards trying to find Krieg on a sideline pattern. They tried the draw again, this time with Zale carrying, but the Steelers wouldn't be fooled twice and it was fourth and a long sixteen at the 35.

He wouldn't whip anybody . . . even the ducks were stepping . . .

Gold dropped back, black helmets butting the gray jerseys away and to the outside, the cup of blockers holding tight. Duvall hooked in the middle and White and Krieg bent to the goalposts and zigged out to the corner flags. White and his man were running stride for stride when Gold let it go, a bad pass, a high, floating balloon of a pass, and the Steeler defensive back must have thought it was Christmas Eve as he turned and saw the ball. He gathered, leaped to tuck it away. But there were only two men in the state who could jump as high as Willie White. Neither of them played football for Fort Steel. It was no contest. White went up for the ball like a man on a trampoline, surging up and up, hanging in the dark air. The leaping Steeler barely reached White's elbows as the end's broad hands closed against the sides of the ball as if it were one of the fifteen or more rebounds he could be counted on to pull down in every basketball game all winter long. When he came down, it was with a touchdown.

Didn't I run good, Daddy? Didn't I?

White casually handed the ball to the chagrined Steeler and walked away. Gold was stopped trying to roll in again for the extra points, but the Owls led for the first time, 14–13.

Why do you do it if you hate it so much?

When the Steeler offensive unit came back on the field, number 11 came with them. "We got 'em," said Muldoon. "Simon can throw, but that's not Fort Steel football." He looked at the clock, sent Krieg and White into the game as cornerbacks.

We'll see how good you run when one of those big . . .

Simon picked up a quick first down on the ground, then went to the air. He hit his first two passes, a quick pop to the left end and a little swing to Strand coming out of the backfield, but the combined gain was barely enough for a first down at the Steeler 38. The crowd came back to life. This was more like it.

how good you run, bub, when one of those big . . .

Simon tried to take advantage then of the fierce rush of Eagle Duvall, setting up a screen to Eagle's side. Rand set as if to block, then tried to slide off Duvall's charge and out into the flat. It was a good call, an excellent call. That is, it would have been an excellent call if anyone could slide off Eagle Duvall and not take a beating. Rand caught a forearm in the chest and shoulder and was still picking himself up when a wide-eyed Simon was going down under Duvall and mountainous Tiny Daugherty. The loss was almost fifteen yards.

Even if you did change, Dale had said, *they'd only see what . . .*

Two plays later Simon threw a hurried square-out at his left end and Billy Krieg came from the inside, tucked the ball in five yards before it reached its intended target, and raced down the sideline for an easy score.

only see what you were. Had been.

Gold passed to Duvall for the extra points and Oiltown had Fort Steel mired deep in its own end of the field when the game ended. Owls 22, Steelers 13.

Off to bed, bub. Off to bed . . .

It seemed silly to take a shower. While his teammates were throwing towels at one another in the steamy locker room, Craig Warren packed his gear and went outside. The dark bus was in the parking lot behind the school, and the driver was joking with two or three Steeler fans and a local policeman. "Thought we had you there at the half," the cop said to the driver as Craig set his bulky equipment bag down by the open luggage compartment. "Shame you didn't throw a few more of those trick passes off the fake field goal."

"Ahhhh. We hadda give ya sump'in," said the driver. "We seen right away ya needed a little help."

Craig got on the bus, made his way to a seat in the rear, and sat looking out at his own reflection in the dark glass. Most of Fort Steel was asleep. The mill ran a full shift on Saturday, and that meant most of the men would have to be up and on their way with their lunch buckets before daylight. Over the shabby roofs of the small city the smokestacks and towers flared against the night sky. Craig thought of a picture in his history book, some European city of tiny clustered houses and rising over them a cathedral like a mountain.

The Owls came out in uproarious bunches of five and six, Muldoon driving and prodding, but his heart not in it. Everything was funny when you won. Almost everything. White was busting up Gold about his throwing, and Gold was taking it well. "Stick with me, babe," Gold crowed. "I can make a receiver out of any pig's ear. Just put out your hands and run. Blind trust, that's what you need. Blind trust."

When the bus started filling up, Craig began to wish he'd taken the shower. If he'd been the last one on, he could have taken the empty seat. This way, somebody had to choose. Muldoon didn't waste the taxpayers' money he kept yapping about. When he chartered a bus, he filled it. The pairing off began: Duvall and Daugherty; Gold and White, still carrying on; Pulaski and Bizarro; then Zale and Billy Krieg. There was a general milling around in the aisles, a jockeying for good position, a window seat away from the coaches but not too near the rough ride over the rear wheels. Craig stared hard at the night and Fort Steel.

"Shove over." It was Eagle Duvall, wearing an enormous scarlet and gray hat with a floppy brim. OWL

PLUCKERS, it said on the band. Scarlet letters on gray. "Whoooeee," he grinned as he settled in. "Ever try to sit next to Daugherty? Like going to bed with a hippopotamus."

Muldoon counted heads. "Move it out," he said to the driver. The bus started to roll. Duvall let his seat slam into its reclining position. "Sorry," he said to the cry of pain from behind him. He nudged the brim of his ridiculous topper down over his eyes. "Now you," he said, "are feeling so puny it's like giving the Eagle two seats to himself. Should've brought along a couple of those little biddy skinny Fort Steel cheerleaders to fill up the empty spaces."

Through the town. A few stoplights, the stores closed, the houses dark. The used-car lots, the cemetery. Then country. Nothing but the dark fields and the road. "Still," said Eagle, just when Craig thought he was asleep, "I always like to see a man be as big as he *can* be, even if it is inconvenient when you're trying to get comfortable on these doggone bus rides."

They rode in silence then. They were halfway back to Oiltown before Craig Warren said, "Eagle, I—" and Duvall interrupted him. "You know what I like about you, Warren? You don't talk shop." And he retilted the hat and settled himself and the matter at the same time.

SIX

Mr. *Craft was reading. The class shifted restlessly,* stretched, drummed fingers, looked out at the September hills. Last period. The hour almost over. "But now go the bells," he read, "and we are ready . . ." There was something funny in his voice, almost as if—"In one house we are sternly stopped / To say we are vexed at her brown study . . ." It was happening. Craig couldn't believe it. He had never seen a man, a grown-up man, cry. He glanced at Dale, feeling as if he might be having hallucinations. No. Mr. Craft had stopped reading and turned to the blackboard. He fished in his coat pocket, took out a handkerchief, and removed his thick glasses. Then he replaced them, put the handkerchief back in his pocket, and turned to face the class. The room hummed with silence. Someone coughed. Laughter echoed down the hall from some other classroom, probably Muldoon's geography class. "To say we are vexed at her brown study, / Lying so primly propped."

"'Bells for John Whiteside's Daughter,'" said Mr. Craft. "Someone else's dead daughter, note, not the daughter of the poet, the narrator. That makes"—he faltered a bit—"that makes a good deal of difference." It was hard to sit and pretend you hadn't seen, pretend everyone hadn't seen.

"First things first, I suppose," Mr. Craft was saying. "Words and the sound of words. The meaning of words after their sound. What does it mean, the phrase *brown study*?" Craig knew. If he had learned nothing else last year from Mrs. Kellogg, he had learned to look up every word in a poem or story he wasn't sure of. A "brown study," the dictionary said, was "a mood of perplexed absorption." He knew all right. Big deal. He wasn't going to put his hand up. Not and get Johnny Zale started on that "Artsy-Craftsy" stuff again. He'd heard a lot of that lately.

The class droned on. Five minutes to go. Less. The autumn sun blew fitfully over the practice field in the distance. "For a week from today," Mr. Craft concluded, "you will write an essay of some five hundred words in which you discuss the meaning and value of any poem found in your textbook." As the bell rang, he added, "The choice of poem, like the discovery of meaning, should be entirely your own." His final sentence was all but lost as the class stampeded for the door.

"What's the rush, Waldo?" Craig said, trying to match Frampton's awkward, almost muscle-bound gait as the reserve lineman made for his locker. Frampton's jaw worked. His square, freckled face was dogged under his thatch of brick-red hair. "Gotta get to practice," he said. "Gotta get ready for Prep."

That's right, Wall-dough," said Johnny Zale, who had come up behind them. "You and Artsy-Craftsy hustle on out there and warm up the ski slope. Maybe Artsy here will be willing to show you his dying chicken passing form. Very big on the road." He sneered. "Understand you were Fort Steel's player of the week," he said to Craig.

Craig tried to laugh it off. "Should've been," he said. "One for one. One pass, one touchdown."

"Terrific," said Johnny Zale. He didn't smile.

At his locker Craig weighed what books to take home. Geography and geometry for sure. Spanish? Yes. Not English. He'd seen what that poetry could do to a man. He dropped the book on the metal locker shelf, slammed the door, and spun the combination lock. He pushed through the heavy double doors of Oiltown High School and started down the gravel path that led round back, past the vocational buildings and to the locker room. Grade-school kids were on their way home.

"Hey, Red! RED! I gotta change my clothes. Meetcha at the nursing home lot in ten minutes!"

"Yeah! You want I should bring my ball?"

"Bring it! An' hurry! We got a dozen guys! *Easy* a dozen!"

Craig stopped, looking back. Clusters of teenagers ambled about, their bright sweaters mirroring the leaves above and around them. Flirting, laughing, pouting, teasing. Chattering in the crisp air. The way home. That was one way. The other way led to the dressing room and beyond that to the practice field and beyond that to the ski slope. The Owl way. The small inflated dummies, the push-backs, that you held against your thigh while the first-stringers smashed your knuckles and stepped on your toes, working on their downfield blocks. The shock —like stuffing your head, neck and shoulders in some giant light socket—if you didn't hit a back like Clint Gold in "good basic football position."

"No, no, no, no, Warren! Bull neck, tail under you, feet

wide and moving! Balance! Balance! Balance!" And get up and do it again. Right.

The way home never seemed so short. The autumn afternoon suddenly seemed to him like one of those big sheets of art paper they gave you when you were a little kid during—what did they call it?—"free time." And you could fill it any way you wanted, any way at all. Craig charged up the front steps, rummaged in the closet under the stairs for his sneaks, grabbed two footballs, one beat-up and scruffy, the other almost new, and hurried out the back door, letting it slam. His mother would be home soon from her job at the music store. She would have to be pleased, Craig thought. It would be hard on his father, but no harder than having to sit through another nightmare like that one in Fort Steel.

He decided he'd make his pretend game harder. By the back porch he kept an old plastic bucket, which he filled with water from his father's hose. Taking the older ball, he dunked it in the bucket, muddied it up a little with the soft dirt alongside the house, then dunked it again. He'd read in a book once how some old-time quarterback had done that, made up rainy days for himself, then practiced until he could throw a wet, muddy ball as well as a dry one.

He enjoyed these imaginary games, a make-believe quarterback fading back under the roar of the crowd, make-believe pass rushers closing in. He looked off the safety, made a head and shoulders fake to his tight end, then fired up the middle to his halfback coming out of the backfield. Bull's-eye! The slippery ball whistled through the tire on the line, and Craig jogged after it. Four out of five and another first down.

"Well, I didn't expect you home." It was his mother, he thought, probably the only lady in town on a warm day like this who would wear a hat and gloves. "Did Mr. Muldoon cancel practice?"

"That'll be the day," said Craig. His mother waited, silent. "No, I just—well, I quit." Still nothing. "I mean," he went on lamely, "all they used me for was holding for extra points, and I even fouled that up. So I just thought —well, maybe—I could use the time to study or something. Anything."

"No," she said. "I won't have it."

He let the muddy football fall to the ground. "I thought you hated football. You've always hated football. Even when I was a little kid—"

"Come in the house," she said, and the door was closed and she was gone.

"I don't get it," he said, entering the kitchen.

"Are you hungry? Would you like some milk?" She put the hat on the top shelf of the closet, standing on tiptoe to do it, then laid her gloves on the scarred top of the desk in the corner. She looked tired.

"I don't get it," Craig said again. "Ever since I can remember you thought football was for jerks, and now when I quit being a jerk, you tell me you won't have it, won't let me quit. What's it to you if I quit?"

She sat down at the kitchen table, the autumn light slanting across her hair and face. "I *don't* hate it," she said. "Not the football. But it's only *one* kind of game. It makes me sad to see so much that's good—so much energy and dedication—go into that kind of play. I just think there are other kinds of play—music drama, literature, art—that are more deserving of that passion for excellence that Mr. Muldoon and the entire city of Oiltown seem to demand only of his athletes."

Sometimes his mother talked like a book. Or like Mr. Craft, which was worse. He tried to tease her out of it. "So

41

I'll dedicate my fabulous energies to something else. Crime-fighting, maybe. Or—what's your favorite charity?"

Mrs. Warren smiled faintly. "You are," she said, "and that's why I'm going to insist you finish what you start. That passion for excellence is worth something in itself, even if it is directed into holding a football for extra punts or field kicks or whatever they are called. If that's what Mr. Muldoon asks you to do, you'll do it as well as you can, at least until you've finished the season you've begun."

"Aw, Mom. Do you mean to tell me I *can't* quit?"

"Well, I would certainly *hope* that you can't." She pushed up from the table with an exaggerated sigh. "Your father will be leaving the refinery and I haven't started supper." She eyed his muddy hands. "How about washing up and peeling some potatoes as long as you're home this once?"

"With energy and dedication?"

"I'll say." She cocked an eyebrow. "That Muldoon never saw the day he was half as mean as I am."

SEVEN

*N*one *of them seemed to notice he had quit. He came* back to find the Owls talking about two things—City Prep, which was natural enough, and Waldo Frampton, which wasn't. Waldo had been a fixture, a kind of stand-up dummy that walked around, ever since his freshman year. You took him for granted, like the ski slope or homework in geometry. But now . . .

It was a favorite drill of Muldoon's. He laid out four tackling dummies to mark a battlefield ten yards long and five yards wide. A tackler was at one end, a ballcarrier at the other. On Muldoon's whistle, Coach Buckwalter would flip the ball to the running back who had to "score" by pounding his way through the dummies that the tackler fought to defend. Five yards didn't give you much space to maneuver in. "Run with abandon!" shouted Muldoon. "Stop babying your precious bodies!" There was a solid *whack* as Eagle Duvall hit Jim DeSales head on and crumpled him back and over. "Ahhhh DeSales, DeSales! He creamed you, DeSales! You wanna dance or you wanna play football? Get out of there before you get hurt!" That was standard Muldoon. The glasses were still on. DeSales was all right.

"Watch him. Watch Waldo," whispered Johnny Zale to the knot of players near the end of the line of ballcarriers. "There he goes!"

Craig watched. Frampton was cheating in the tacklers' line. He was gazing intently at the ballcarriers, his lips moving as he counted runners, and then he moved up two players, shoving in abruptly in front of Tiny Daugherty. Daugherty looked surprised, then, with an enormous giggle, he pointed to Waldo's calves. "Last time I saw a pair of legs like those, Frampton," he said, "they had a message attached to 'em. Get it, Pulaski?" he chortled. "I mean like one of those messenger pigeons or something." He dug an elbow painfully into Pulaski's ribs. Daugherty fancied himself the team comedian, and he hated to laugh alone.

"Listen to old Waldo," snickered Zale. "Hear it?"

Frampton was starting to growl, a low rumbling, the ridiculous house pet gone berserk. Players were trying to keep from laughing. Billy Krieg juked around Larry Bizarro, going between the dummies almost untouched, and Muldoon came down hard on Bizarro. They did it again, and this time Bizarro stopped Krieg cold and Muldoon was on his speedy flanker. "Come on, Krieg, come *on!* You won't always have nothing in front of you but grass. What if you'd had to beat a *man* down there at Fort Steel?"

And then Craig saw what Frampton was after. It was Clint Gold. He must have gone crazy, Craig thought. "Weren't you just up?" Muldoon asked Frampton.

"No sir." Frampton lied so blatantly that even Muldoon grinned behind his hand.

"That's funny," said Muldoon, "since Gold, Zale and White have run twice apiece, and you've been here to tackle 'em every time. Not to mention one or two other assaults in between."

"Yessir," said Frampton. "Guess our line is shorter." That one was so patently untrue that everybody cracked up.

"Well, it's your funeral," said Muldoon, and he blew the whistle.

Buckwalter flipped the ball to Gold, and the big back churned forward, knees and elbows pumping. Frampton lunged awkwardly, hit, bounced off, lunged again, grabbed a leg, crawled and reached to get the other leg, tugged and hauled and pulled and finally wrestled Gold to the ground. He was a yard short of the dummies that marked paydirt. Muldoon's glasses came off. "Look at yourself, Gold," he bellowed. "Look at yourself! That's three times you've carried against Frampton. Three times. So far you've made it once. One lousy time! The great Clint Gold! Scores one, throws for one against Fort Steel! You memorize those headlines? Boy, I bet City Prep is laughing! Now get up and beat this man, or I'll find a quarterback who can!"

Gold's thick neck turned crimson and he stormed back to the head of the line. Craig felt sorry for Frampton. Waldo had started to growl again, a throaty purr that seemed too big to be coming from him. Muldoon blasted the whistle and Gold exploded like a bull coming out of a chute. This time Frampton shot forward with his nose almost on the ground and he hit Gold at the shins with an impact that flipped the big senior completely in the air and landed him on his back. Gold leaped to his feet and threw the ball at Frampton as the scrub lineman was turning to get up. The ball narrowly missed and Frampton was after it like a terrier on a rat, scattering the line of ballcarriers as he dove headlong, and then rolled over and over with what he must have taken to be a fumble.

Muldoon stared at Clint Gold for what seemed like a full minute. Gold couldn't take that. He looked down, scuffed dirt with his cleats. And into the tension walked Waldo Frampton, carrying the football like a carefully wrapped birthday present. "Here, sir," he said to Muldoon.

Muldoon's jaw dropped. For a second or two he was speechless. But only for a second or two. "Just recover them, Waldo," he said dryly. "You don't have to turn them in to me."

"I really get a kick out of that Frampton," said Coach Buckwalter in the tiny cubicle where the coaches dressed and showered after practices.

"Like a new kid," said Gene Dykstra, the line coach.

"Well, he got himself a heart transplant someplace," said Muldoon. "You have to wait on these things to see if they take, but when they do, they make this coaching racket the best there is."

"That's right," said Dykstra. "I just wish it would happen to some of these kids with more physical ability."

"Amen to that," said Muldoon.

Through the thin walls the coaches could hear the Owls' subdued horseplay after the long practice. Enough years on the job and you could tell everything about a team's closeness and mental readiness just by the noise coming from another room. "One thing's sure," Buckwalter sighed. "No worries about overconfidence this week."

46

"No," said Muldoon.

"It's the papers," said Dykstra. "These kids keep reading how *big* Prep is. Some of our linemen, the newer kids like Pulaski and Bizarro, let it get to them. Even Bates and Thomas."

"Not the size of the dog in the fight," said Buckwalter.

"Prep's always big," said Muldoon. "Big, fancy, and soft. Get those kids of theirs in shape, they'd weigh less than our line does."

"They got that nose guard goes almost three hundred pounds," said Dykstra.

"Yes," said Muldoon. "That reminds me." He clomped out of the coaches' room in his old gray sweatsuit, strode through the equipment room with the shelves of polished black helmets, hangers of black on white and white on black jerseys, piles of cleated shoes, the smell of leather, and stood in the door of the Owl locker room. The players, in various stages of undress, grew quiet.

"Just a reminder," Muldoon said, polishing his glasses. "Bonfire and pep rally Thursday night. Be there!"

There were loud groans from all corners.

"I know," said Muldoon. "Some of you'd rather play Prep barefoot than go to a pep rally. Well, I don't like 'em myself. But the bonfire before the first home game's a tradition so old nobody remembers when it started. And the town likes it, and the alumni like it, and the cheerleaders and the pom-pom girls and the band like it. And my boss, the principal, likes it." Muldoon looked around. "And I have to make a speech, and that means *you'll* like it."

"Hey, none of us wants to miss *that*, Coach," said Eagle Duvall, deadpan.

"Lordy, no," said Willie White.

47

Muldoon grinned, hiding it as usual behind his fist. "Thank you, boys," he said. Then the grin was gone. "Be there," he said.

Drums thundered in the distance and the sky was bright with stadium lights beyond the rooftops of the low houses and the higher roof of the nursing home. It reminded Craig Warren of nights so long ago that he could barely remember them or maybe only remember when he *did* remember. When he passed Dale Davis's house, Dale was coming down the steps. "Going to the rally?" she asked.

"Or else," Craig said.

The leaves were bright yellow under the streetlights as they made their way across the street toward the faint sounds of band music.

Craig glanced at Dale furtively. *Something* had sure happened to her in the past year. Rumor had it that she was even getting the rush from the great Clint Gold himself—that he'd asked her out twice, been turned down twice. A lot of the senior girls thought Dale was grandstanding, but she didn't seem to know what they thought—or care if she did.

"Don't you just love it?" Dale said. "Football season, pep rallies?"

"Love which?" said Craig. "Football's football. This is something else."

"But don't you see? It's all part of the same thing."

"There's football," said Craig Warren, "and there's pep rallies. I'm good at pep rallies."

There was a fire truck parked near the stadium fence and not far from the huge pile of wood that included an old rowboat and a picket fence, standing in the center of the parking lot. The band was there, not in uniform but blasting away on their instruments in a kind of undisciplined and happy jam session. The cheerleaders in their black-and-white sweaters and short, pleated skirts flirted indiscriminately; and the players stood in small clusters, looked embarrassed, and tried not to seem pleased. Among the townspeople, Joe Hugo and the rest of the downtown quarterbacks made a separate group and talked in low voices from the sides of their mouths. The schoolgirls milled around like bright birds, chattering happily in their new fall outfits.

After a while the band took over and played the famous victory marches, Notre Dame's, Michigan's, "On Wisconsin," "On Brave Old Army Team." They played Penn State's march, too, which was not famous but which was a favorite of the band director's because he had gone there. Next came the cheerleaders, kicking high as they went through their repertoire, their mouths making perfect O's as they spelled out OWLS under the cold lights. Then it was Muldoon's turn. He stood on a small platform against the stadium fence. Behind him a huge sign proclaimed THIS IS OWL COUNTRY. The band blasted a fanfare, and everyone grew quiet.

"Good to see you out here," said Muldoon. "All of you. Students, alumni, faculty, the band, the yell leaders, yesterday's Owls—especially yesterday's Owls, players who've graduated and still come back to support their team every year. That connects us all. That's what tradition means."

Craig glanced over at the knot of older men standing in the shadows. Fat Joe Hugo. Quick Keller. Others he didn't know. It must be strange, he thought, to be out of all this, to remember the ski slope and the band music all

49

mixed together with ten or twenty games from fifteen years ago. If the men were moved by Coach Muldoon's words, they didn't show it. They stared carefully into space or at the ground.

"Anyway," Muldoon went on, "all of you being here like this tonight makes me feel real good, and it makes the team feel good, too. So I'm going to do something I've never done before." Muldoon took off his glasses. His voice took on some of its practice field anger. "I'm going to make a prediction. I predict we're going to win this game. And I'm going to tell you why.

"Some of you read the papers, and if you do, you've been reading how BIG City Prep is, 'the massive front five' and all that malarky. Well, I'm here to tell you I like my players lean and mean and hungry. I don't like 'em fat. I don't like a lineman so soft a back can run into him and gain five yards before coming to a backbone. That's why we run the ski slope. That's why we run more than any team in this state to get ready for a season, to get ready for these games. And that's why we'll beat City Prep tomorrow night."

Muldoon paused. "I guarantee it!" he said, and the crowd roared. Muldoon waited for silence, milked the moment fully. "Because," he said, "if we *don't* win after I've gone and promised we would, we'll just have to do some *extra* running till we're a whole lot nastier."

The Owls knew what that meant. Duvall raised a clenched fist shoulder high, and the others nodded solemnly.

Then the fire was lit and the flames leaped toward the black September sky. The smell of wood smoke filled the crisp night air. The cheerleaders joined hands and everyone sang the alma mater:

Mid the hills of Pennsylvania
Stands the school we love;
Our devotion is as steadfast
As the stars above.

Some knew as they sang that it was corny, but it was also a sweet moment, the old voices and the young voices blending together in one of the few songs both groups knew by heart. Then it was time to go home.

"Muldoon's not as bad as I thought," said Dale. "Sometimes he's pretty funny, all that about running five yards into a fat man."

"He's funny, all right," said Craig Warren. "That ski slope is a million laughs."

Blocks away, on a darker street, Joe Hugo and a small group of the former Owls were making their way toward the heart of the town, the bar at the Oiltown Hotel. "Rallies ain't what they used to be," one of them said.

"Used to be bigger," said Quick Keller.

"What was?" said another Owl.

"Everything," said Keller. "Crowds, bonfires, even the City Prep line. Remember, Joey H? One time we had a whole entire chicken coop somebody stole and dumped on that woodpile."

"Ahhh, boys," said Joe Hugo. "Don't you see? It's the same size it always was. You get far enough away from it, everything looks smaller than it did then."

They walked the rest of the way without saying much. The shadows of the dark hills rose above them, and above the hills the steadfast September stars.

EIGHT

The buses that brought the City Prep football team, band, and pep club through the red-and-gold-leaved fall hills the next afternoon were new and air-conditioned and had tinted glass, and the automobiles that filled the visitors' section of the parking lot were expensive and heavy with chrome. One of the buses had a banner hanging from the side windows. It read GO BARONS: STICK THE HICKS! The sign was not wasted on the Owls as they made their way in groups of two and three into the locker room that evening.

Muldoon had little to say for once, and the Owls were quiet as they dressed in front of the gray lockers that had their names in tape on the wire mesh doors. He simply pulled out the heavy chalkboard from the equipment room and drew once again the blocking assignments for the new series of trap plays he and Buckwalter and Dykstra had put in for Prep.

"Any questions?" There were none. "All right, gentlemen," said Muldoon. "Saddle up." The Owls took down their shoulder pads from the locker hooks, put them on, wrestled on the white game jerseys with the black numbers front and back, put on their helmets. Muldoon lifted an eyebrow. "Stick the hicks, eh? Well, hicks, let's get on out there."

It was the first time Craig Warren had ever run out on the field of Owl Stadium for a home game. He felt weak. The noise, the lights, the music seemed to fall on him with unexpected weight. Suddenly he was staggered by an enormous whack on his shoulder pads. Craig turned, and there was Eagle Duvall. Eagle was smiling broadly. "C'mon, Warren," he said. "It isn't a trial or a funeral or anything. It's a game, remember? It's what you do for fun." Then Duvall trotted off. Across the way City Prep gathered around their coach, but with none of the kamikaze spirit that had characterized Fort Steel a week before. The Barons were huge and confident and sophisticated as they trotted into position to kick off.

"It figures they'd want to kick," Muldoon said to Buckwalter. "Get those defensive monsters out there early and force a mistake."

The Prep kicker drilled the ball high into the night air and Johnny Zale took it in full stride at his own 15. Two or three of the Barons got downfield at less than full speed, and it left gaps in their coverage as Zale started up the middle and suddenly shifted gears to cut into a hole to his left. The crowd screamed as he shook loose from an arm tackle at his own 35 and found himself running free with only the kicker to beat. Johnny Zale was a smart runner, too smart to help the kicker by giving him the sideline as a teammate. He cut back to the center of the field, got a block from Mark Thomas, and then he was running all alone while the drums rattled and the Owl fans shrieked with delight. Muldoon loved it. "All right, hicks!" he yelped. Gold tacked on the extra point out of Krieg's hold, and the Owls led 7–0 with less than a half minute gone.

Prep's attack was like their green uniforms—fancy. They came out in a spread formation the first time they had the ball. The quarterback dropped deep, then threw a screen pass to a halfback near the sideline and the halfback in turn heaved a fifty-yard bomb to his lanky split end cutting deep across the field. It might have been a touchdown, except Mulldoon had warned the Owls to expect some kind of razzle-dazzle early on, and Billy Krieg was running with the Baron receiver stride for stride. They went up together and came down together, but Krieg had the ball.

The Owls started again, this time from their own 30. Time and time again, Gold would take a jab step right or left, fake to DeSales or Zale, then reverse quickly and slip the ball to the second back through going the opposite direction. The big Prep nose guard would be leaning one way and the guards, Thomas or Bizarro, would keep him going. That freed the center, Pulaski, to block the smaller linebackers.

"Just like a big green marble in a football hat," Muldoon said exultantly. "Get that nose guard rolling one direction, he just keeps rolling till it thunders."

It was a picture-perfect drive, textbook football, the Owls getting more than five yards a crack against much bigger players. Once Clint Gold dropped back to pass and overthrew Billy Krieg at the sideline, but the frustrated nose guard took out his annoyance on Gold after the throw, and the Owls got a fifteen-yard gift from the roughing-the-passer penalty. DeSales slammed up the middle for the final three yards and the Owls' second touchdown. Gold knocked through the extra point and the home team was off to a 14–0 lead.

Prep was too talented to bottle up all night, and their

quarterback could throw far better than Clint Gold. Passing on first downs, running just enough to keep the Owls honest, he moved his team deep into Oiltown territory as the quarter ended. There, however, on successive downs Eagle Duvall beat his blocker badly. The first time the quarterback went down for a twelve-yard loss, and got up barking at his guilty teammate. When Duvall slipped inside the blocker a second time, the Prep lineman resorted to a shoestring tackle to keep the Eagle from dismembering his quarterback. It would have taken a blind man not to have seen the infraction, and the backfield judge was not blind. The holding penalty took City Prep out of scoring position, and they wound up punting the ball away.

Once again the Owls began a drive, this time with more difficulty. With a little more than a minute to go in the half, they were stymied with a third-and-eight situation just inside the midfield stripe. Gold called time out and trotted over to talk with Muldoon.

The Owls lined up with Eagle Duvall to the right side. Gold pivoted to his right and put the ball in Johnny Zale's stomach as Zale followed Jim DeSales hard into the off-tackle hole between Duvall and Tiny Daugherty. City Prep had had enough of Johnny Zale, and they reacted quickly to plug the gap. But Zale didn't take the ball. Instead, Gold took it from Zale's stomach and slipped it to Eagle Duvall, who had hesitated a count and then drove down along the line to his left while Gold continued on around the right end. Prep's nose guard surged toward Johnny Zale and was still puffing and grunting on top of the tough little running back when Duvall broke through the middle of the Prep defense, cut back against the flow of green-shirted pursuit, and raced along the left sideline toward the end zone. The Prep safety man met Duvall head-on at the 5 yard line, but they were both lying well inside paydirt with cheers and music floating down from the stands when the play ended. Duvall helped the Baron defensive back to his feet. "Tell the truth now," said Eagle. "Isn't life better in the country?"

Gold converted a third time, and at the half the Owls were coasting.

Craig Warren stood on the sideline with the rest of the reserves, all of them cheering like maniacs, and watched the second half with amazement. The Owls were like a bunch of kids throwing an old football around in a vacant lot on a Saturday morning. They were revved up, moving so quickly it seemed they had all the time in the world to make the moves a football team makes, running the ball down the field. Prep defenders seemed to topple in slow motion; holes opened like castle doors in horror movies and gaped there as if they would never close again; Owl ballcarriers took in the secondary at a glance, then exploded in unpredictable, yard-busting directions. Craig couldn't believe it. Eagle Duvall was right. The Owls were having *fun*. When Johnny Zale dove over a tangle of blockers and hapless Barons for his second touchdown of the night, Craig dared a quick glance at Muldoon, half-hoping the feisty coach might give him a chance to redeem himself, as a holder for place kicks at least. But Muldoon's eyes were riveted to the field, and Billy Krieg's sure hands placed the ball while Clint Gold kicked the extra point squarely between the uprights and clear out onto the running track behind the end zone. And then Muldoon began running his second unit into the game.

The Owls who came out of the battle were elated, slapping palms elaborately, begging Muldoon for "just one more series." The players who hadn't gotten in were popping each other on the pads and helmets, doing shoulder rolls along the sideline, anything to catch the eye of one of the coaches. Even the second unit couldn't miss. A disgruntled Prep back coughed up the football early in the fourth quarter, and the reserves managed to drive it the twenty necessary yards for a score. Muldoon took a satisfied glance at the scoreboard, polished his glasses to be sure he was reading the 35–0 correctly, and started sending in new players in waves. With only a few minutes left, he ran his eye along the bench and grinned. "Frampton," he said. "Get on in there and play an inside linebacker."

Waldo went bounding onto the field, his red cowlick flapping with each ungainly stride, and the Owls promptly had to take a time-out while Frampton returned, red-faced, to the bench for his helmet. The first unit loved it. "Way to go, Wall-dough!"

The Baron quarterback hadn't completely given up. He'd known for some time that his team wasn't going back to the city with a win, but there was still time to pile up some personal statistics, maybe catch some college scout's eye. With that in mind, ignoring field position, he kept throwing the football.

"I'll give you five dollars," Muldoon said to Coach Buckwalter, "if you can tell me what position Frampton's playing."

Buckwalter chuckled. "Coach, I can't even tell you what *game* he's playing."

Waldo was lining up in a different place for each snap of the ball, sometimes outside an end, sometimes almost back in with the safety man, occasionally as if by accident in roughly the area usually occupied by linebackers. Whatever his starting position, each time the ball was snapped he charged off like an overwound wind-up toy, bouncing off teammates and opponents alike in his effort to be someplace on the green-and-white tangle that ended every play.

With seconds left in the game, the Prep quarterback dropped back one last time into his own end zone, looking downfield for an open receiver. They were all covered, and none of them seemed too interested in sprinting an additional fifteen yards back upfield to serve as a release man. The quarterback did the only thing he *could* do, simply took off. Getting outside an overanxious scrub end, he ran for the left sideline. At least he could make the flag, get out of the end zone, and save himself two last ignominious points. He hadn't counted on Waldo Frampton. Growling and snarling, running awkwardly, his chin almost plowing grass, Waldo was racing the rangy Baron to the corner flag. They met with a solid *whack* at the goal line. The collision was all but drowned out by a roar from the watching Owls; the quarterback sailed out of bounds and the ball rolled free in the end zone. The referee finally gave up trying to untangle the swarm of white jerseys and black helmets that piled onto each other and the ball. He just took the whistle from his mouth, shrugged, and shot his arms in the air. Touchdown!

"Well, I'll be!" said Muldoon.

It seemed to Craig Warren that he had turned up at the junior prom all decked out in a rented tuxedo, only to find that the class had voted to turn the affair into a combination square dance and hog call. Delirium was the word for the night, and Craig hadn't gotten the word. The Owls were flying high. Tape, white jerseys, T-shirts, towels and socks floated in the air like snow. Everyone had a badge of courage, a raw mud and grass stain on the jersey, a scraped shin, a raw knuckle, or a daub of Prep green on the black helmet.

Waldo Frampton came in for a lot of back and shoulder thumping and for a minute or two Eagle Duvall led a "Way to go, Wall-dough" chant that was, like everything Eagle did, half a joke and half serious, a way of making Waldo feel like a hero. Waldo's face, always flushed with intensity, was glowing. The coaches wandered among the players, shaking hands and saying, "Nice job, nice job," again and again. Coach Buckwalter slapped Craig on the shoulder. "Good game," he said. Then he noticed Craig's uniform, the only laundry-fresh all-white jersey in the room. "Didn't we get you in there?" he asked. Craig shook his head. "It's a long season," said Coach Buckwalter. "You'll get your chance."

Once again, there was no point in showering. Craig packed his gear in his locker, dressed quickly, and went outside. It was a clear night. Leaves were falling and drifting over the litter of game programs scattered at the edges of the parking lot. A cluster of Oiltown High students—some cheerleaders, the Key Clubbers who had worked at the concession stand, Dale Davis and some of her friends—were standing in front of the darkened schoolhouse.

"Nice game, Craig," sang out one of the cheerleaders as he passed.

"Yeah," said one of the Key Clubbers, "really nice."

And as he walked by, Dale Davis reached out and, so quickly that afterward he was almost not sure it had happened, gave his arm a squeeze. It helped. But not enough.

NINE

The beginning of October. Saturday, bright and blue. The downtown quarterbacks gathered early, and the whole town speeded up with excitement.

"Hey, Joey H," said one of the younger ex-Owls, Dude Perenchio, "did you read the *Journal* this morning?"

Hugo said nothing. He had read it and reread it, but it was worth hearing Perenchio read it again.

"Listen to this," said Perenchio, and the crowd pressed in, reading over his shoulder. " 'Showing no mercy in any quarter, the Oiltown Owls last night rode roughshod over an overconfident and somewhat bloated lineup of City Prep Barons. The Owls, led by Johnny Zale who blasted for one hundred fifty-seven yards on twenty-three carries, made the previously unbeaten Prepsters look as if they were on rollerskates in piling up a forty-one to zero victory.' "

"I *saw* the game," said Joe Hugo. "Tell me something I don't know."

"Read him Carl Carmen's column, Dude," said Quick Keller.

"Yeah, right," said Perenchio, rattling the *Journal* and folding it over. "How about *this?* 'Last night's convincing victory over a highly regarded and previously unscored-upon City Prep squad is bound to give the Owls their highest ranking in many years in state football circles. Pre-season prognosticators had picked Oiltown to be among the top ten teams, and last night's overwhelming victory, coupled with losses by Allenville and Port Worden from the Pittsburgh area, make the Owls almost certain to find themselves somewhere in the top five when the polls come out late in the week. Among the Owls' future opponents, only Brackenridge, led by the phenomenal do-everything tailback, Mike Michelonis, is likely to be ranked as high. The Owls will have to take a lesson from City Prep and resist overconfidence, especially next weekend, when they travel south to McKean to take on a young and undermanned Bulldog squad.' "

"Think of it," said Quick Keller. "Top five in the state. Why, we ain't been that high in *years.*"

"Thirty-one years, to be exact," said Joe Hugo, shifting his weight and spitting with the wind.

"Was that your year, Joe?" asked Dude Perenchio.

Hugo nodded. "How high'd you guys finish?" asked Keller.

"*Finished* fourth," said Hugo. "Fourth at the end of the year, after the chickens are in the sack, fourth when it counts. Lost one game by one point to Oldfield."

"Wow, that's tough," said someone in the crowd.

Joe Hugo said nothing, looking past everyone to the hills and fall trees and remembering an extra point try that sailed wide one night a half a lifetime ago.

"Well, these kids got a chance," someone said.

"I'll say."

"If they don't get big heads."

"That's right. If they keep their helmets on right."

"That's all that can beat 'em, is overconfidence."

Joe Hugo looked around the circle scornfully. "While you bozos were reading the *Journal* and spouting off all those statistics about so many yards on so many carries, I don't expect any of you noticed this statistic here." He reached out and seized the paper from Perenchio, refolded it, and pointed a crooked finger to a line of print. "Read that!" he said.

The line read, "Passes attempted 11/Passes completed 1."

"Heck, we don't hardly need to pass," said Perenchio. "Duvall and Daugherty knocking people down like they are, and Zale running."

"Sooner or later," said Hugo, "a football team has to get balance."

"That'll come," someone said.

"And while we're talking," said Joe Hugo, "we still got to get past Brackenridge, and that Michelonis runs like a badger in a forest fire."

"He ain't that big," said Keller. "What is he? Maybe six foot, a hundred seventy-five?"

"Ain't all that *fast*, either," said Perenchio. "They say he plays baseball 'stead of track 'cause he ain't but about the fifth or sixth fastest runner Brackenridge has."

"Doesn't throw all that well, for all the big fuss over him," said another man, one who had been a quarterback for the Owls a decade before. "Last year, that pass that beat us down there? Wobbled like my mother-in-law in high-heeled shoes."

"It got there, didn't it?" Joe Hugo reminded everyone. "That's the thing. There are maybe faster players, and lots of bigger ones. I guess there's better passers and better kickers someplace, though when the game's on the line, I

doubt it. Thing is," Joe said, "Michelonis has got it *here*."
He tapped his heart lightly. He smiled. "He's like the
players in the *old* days is what he is. Whatever he is, he's
the last of his kind."

"Any questions?" asked Mr. Craft, closing his book and
smiling. He had been teaching a poem by Emily Dickinson. "Success is counted sweetest," it began, "By those
who ne'er succeed."

Craig Warren had questions all right, and about success, but not for Emily Dickinson, and not for Mr. Craft.
He had been fidgeting for forty minutes, waiting for the
bell. At last it rang, and Craig was up and out the door,
waiting. When Waldo Frampton ambled out, Craig
moved in. "How's it going, Waldo?" he asked.

"Fine," said Waldo. "Good, real good."

The halls were full of Owl Fever. Banners were everywhere. WHO'S AFRAID OF THE BIG BAD WOLF?
and OWLS EAT UP WOLFBURGERS. Kids dressed in
black and white swirled out of the classrooms and banged
their locker doors open and shut getting ready to go
home.

"Hey, you goin' Friday night?"

"Gotta ride?"

And nobody needed to ask where they were going or
why a ride was needed. The Owls were ranked number
five in the whole state, and everybody wanted to see them
cream McKean's Wolves.

Craig had to hustle to keep up with Waldo as they made
their way through the crowds. "Waldo," he said, "hey,
tell me something, okay?"

"Sure," said Waldo, pushing doggedly ahead. "Just so
we can move and talk at the same time. Gotta get to
practice on time."

"Right, sure," said Craig. "What I want to know is, well, what *happened?*"

"Happened when?" asked Waldo. He was at his locker now, rummaging around in a clutter of books, candy wrappers, abandoned scarves and earmuffs, and crumpled sheets of looseleaf paper.

Craig sighed. Waldo could be exasperating. Maybe he *didn't* know. Maybe he had just changed, woke up a new person and didn't even remember the old. "Look," said Craig. "I've known you what—two or three years now? You've always been, well, you know, not a very good football player, kind of slow and—well, you know. And now, all of a sudden . . ."

Waldo turned around and squinted shrewdly at Craig. His red face looked indecisive for a moment. Then he took Craig by the arm and pulled him close. He glanced quickly to either side. Then, satisfied no one could hear anything in the after-school din, he whispered a single word: "Physics!"

"Physics?" Craig exclaimed loudly, and Waldo shushed him elaborately. He waved his stubby arms, and looked around. Then he pulled Craig into one of the small alcoves leading to an abandoned classroom. "Promise you won't tell anyone else? Not Zale? Not even Eagle?"

Craig nodded.

"I'll tell *you*, Craig. You never laughed at me much—even before—and you're not really like those other guys."

Craig sighed again. "Isn't *that* the truth." Then he frowned. "But *physics?*"

"Physics," said Waldo. "It's mass times velocity squared. Remember? Mr. Clark taught that a couple weeks ago."

"Yeah. Maybe. I dunno. Physics? I study for the tests, but . . . *What's* mass times the square of velocity?"

"No, no," said Waldo. "Mass times velocity *squared.* That's *momentum.* Remember now? Momentum? Like the coaches are always talking about *momentum?*"

Craig looked at Waldo's freckled face with its comic, almost invisible reddish eyebrows and intense, half-crazy blue eyes, and he wanted to laugh. Or maybe cry. So that was Waldo's great secret. "It's not the same, Waldo," he said. "Mr. Clark and the coaches, it's not the same kind of momentum."

"Momentum's momentum," said Waldo, setting his jaw. "You asked me, I told you. My dad, he used to be a chief petty officer in the Navy, he showed me. Momentum's momentum, no matter what."

Waldo was off again, trudging as fast as he could in the direction of the locker room. Craig tagged along. "Wait a minute. Waldo! Darn it, Waldo, just one more minute!"

Waldo stopped. "You were making fun," he said.

"No. Well, maybe. A little." Waldo turned to go. "Wait, Waldo. I'm sorry. I really want to know. *How* did your dad show you? *What* did he show you?"

"It's mass times velocity *squared.* It's the squared factor that counts most. With matchsticks on the kitchen table is how he showed it. It was like an experiment."

"An experiment?"

It was Waldo's turn to sigh. "Craig, if you keep saying everything over after I say it, we'll *never* get to practice. My dad took out these matchsticks and he showed me how, if two of 'em run together, the one that's going slowest is the one that breaks. That's momentum. So if you're going fastest, you don't get hurt. See? My dad says it's why bullets hurt more than clubs."

For a moment it all seemed simple. Waldo, or Waldo's father, was a genius. Then Craig said, "What if a fast toothpick runs into a slow club, or a baseball bat?"

65

Waldo frowned. "I'll ask my dad," he said. Then, as the other Oiltown kids moved around them on the way home, he added, "Some things, Craig, it's good to think about, but not *too* much, if you see what I mean. If you think about something just enough, then sometimes it helps."

"My trouble," Craig said, "is I can't stop thinking. My imagination's too good. I keep imagining Gold's knees, or those crazies down at Fort Steel. I even dream about 'em. Every time I go to make a tackle or something, I imagine what could happen if—"

"I'm not much at imagining things," said Waldo. "Come on, Muldoon will run us till dark if we're late."

The scout team, decked out in orange scrimmage vests, was trying to run McKean's winged-T offense against the first string. Craig Warren was glad he wasn't handling the ball. Al Hanson, a senior, had moved ahead of him even though Hanson couldn't pass at all and was a clumsy ball handler. Muldoon was driving everyone hard. "What's the matter, DeSales, been staying up nights reading your clippings?" Nobody was spared. Muldoon was worried.

Waldo Frampton was working as a scout team guard, pulling awkwardly and chugging down the line time and again, trying to block for McKean's sweep or off-tackle plays. Most of the time Daugherty and White and Duvall simply overpowered their smaller orange-shirted opponents and the running backs shuttled in and out for the scout team so that nobody had to suffer too many times in a row.

"All right, one more time," said Muldoon for about the tenth time. The scout team huddled around Coach Buckwalter, looking at the McKean off-tackle play which he had drawn up on a big cardboard sheet. It was basic football, the end and tackle double-teaming the defensive tackle, the guard pulling down the line and driving the end to the outside, the first back through the hole blocking the linebacker, and the second back carrying the ball.

The scouts broke the huddle. Hanson called signals, mimicking McKean's irregular starting count. When the ball was snapped, the scouts came off raggedly, but Waldo Frampton shot down the line and smashed into the defensive end with enough force to bounce the larger player a yard or so away from the play. The double-team block held, for once, and the scrub running back found himself with the first hole he'd seen in over a week. He accelerated through it, cut to the middle of the field, and picked up about a dozen yards before Pulaski hooked his jersey and pads from behind and pulled him down.

Muldoon was thunderstruck. Waving his glasses, he moved in on the hapless defensive end. "Son," he yelled, "what kind of play is that? You see that double-team, you *feel* that double-team on Daugherty, you've *got* to close down on that hole! You've got to *meet* that guard, not tiptoe up and give him a kiss! Down at McKean Friday night, they'll *really* be coming down that line and they've got a guard who'll knock you on your teacup if you don't get ready to hit somebody! Let's see it again! Same play."

The scout team exchanged anxious glances. It was bad enough, running at Daugherty and Pulaski and the rest, but when Muldoon was chewing them out and when they knew what was coming, the Owl first unit was outright nasty. "I think I hear my mother calling me," said the reserve back who had just survived with a twelve-yard gain.

"Cut that talk," said Coach Buckwalter. "We're here to help. Here's the play. Everybody got a look? Okay? On two."

The scout team moved slowly up to the ball. On the snap, Daugherty reacted violently into the double-team, throwing off the scrub end and tackle like pygmies. The varsity end closed into the tackle hole at top speed. But once again Frampton shot along the line, this time lower than the time before, and he managed to get a solid block on the taller boy's shins, tumbling him into Daugherty. All went down in a heap, and the reserve back skipped nimbly outside the pile, romped five yards and escaped out of bounds, grinning with relief.

Muldoon couldn't believe it. He stared at his guilty end while all the Owls grew quiet. "Hell's bells!" he snapped. "I'm an old man and I'm not wearing pads or a helmet, and I can play a better defensive end than that! Close it *down!* Strike that guard a blow!" He whipped off his rimless glasses. "Here, hold these!" he said to Coach Dykstra. He pushed the end roughly to the sideline. "This is what I want," he said, lining up in the end's defensive place. Then, to Buckwalter, "Run it again, Bill."

Some of the Owls grinned, being careful that Muldoon didn't see. Muldoon did this a half-dozen times a year, got himself in a fever and couldn't stand it any longer but had to jump in and bang around in a scrimmage. None of them could quite bring himself to go full speed on a coach, a gray-haired man in a rumpled sweatsuit, playing without a helmet, so Muldoon had things pretty much his way. It was hard on the scout team, because when Muldoon was trying to demonstrate how to play "with abandon," he could get pretty rough.

Once again the scouts came over the ball. With the snap, Muldoon shot forward and he and Waldo slammed together. The Owls couldn't believe it. Frampton, that crazy Waldo, had gone into Muldoon full tilt. Daugherty and the rest of the Owl line stopped the ballcarrier, but

Frampton was lying on Muldoon's chest and Buckwalter and Dykstra looked as if they were going to bust something, trying not to laugh.

At last Coach Dykstra walked over and offered Muldoon a hand up. "You okay, Coach?"

"Hell's bells," said Muldoon. " 'Course I'm all right." He whirled to face the sidelined defensive end, whose expression changed magically from eye-watering amusement to a look of concern for his coach's well-being. "Son," he snapped, "I sure hope you were watching, because that's how *football* is played! The way Frampton played it! Full bore! I'm an old man and I'm in sweats, and *still* I closed down better than you. But Frampton was playing the game."

The end studied his cleats. "Yessir," he said.

"And as for *you*, Frampton," said Muldoon, turning to face the stumpy lineman, "as for you . . ." The Owls waited. Nobody had ever made Muldoon look bad before. "You just earned yourself a seat—on the bus to McKean."

Eagle Duvall slipped Willie White a wink. So Waldo Frampton had made the traveling squad by upending the coach. Allll right!

TEN

C*raig Warren had earned himself a seat, too—in one* of the chairs in his mother's kitchen, staring at the yellow-flowered wallpaper and trying to coax the play-by-play report of the Owls' game with McKean through the static and competing stations of the family's old Philco radio. "Sure you don't want to ride down to McKean and have a look?" his father had asked two or three times. Craig was sure. Nonetheless, he kept shifting the dials, trying to get Carl Carmen's voice to come in clearly, trying to avoid another, more excited voice broadcasting some other game with players' names that meant nothing to Craig.

Even under ideal listening conditions, even when reception was perfect, Craig knew Carl Carmen's account of a football game bore little resemblance to reality. Carmen was famous for his account of the Oldfield game a few years back when he credited Oldfield's star linebacker with sixteen tackles. It turned out the player had missed the game altogether with a leg injury. Mostly, when the Owls had the ball, he had the ballcarrier right, but he just

70

ran a stubby finger down the opponents' lineup and gave the tackle to the name nearest his fingernail. Still, despite Carl Carmen's bumbling account of the game, augmented by color commentary from Gabby Rawley, one thing was clear. Oiltown was having unexpected trouble with the McKean Wolves.

"Well, Gabby," Carmen was saying, "how about these young Wolves? Who would have thought they'd hold the Oiltown Owls to a nothing-nothing tie after a full half of football?"

"Right you are, Carl," said Gabby. "This is a young team, but they really came to play tonight. They're flat out getting after people and, when you look down that lineup, look at those sophomores and juniors, even a freshman or two getting playing time, well, you just have to think McKean is going to be tough in years to come."

"Gabby, I think that hits it right square between the nose. This is a team that has its whole future right in front of it, and that's what makes high school football the great spectacle that it is. But what about the Owls? What is Coach Muldoon saying to them down in that locker room right now?"

Static broke in, a crackling like thunder, then a sound like a bosun's pipe, and a voice screaming, "Michelonis hit *hard* at the line of scrimmage, falls forward for a pickup of maybe a yard!"

Annoyed, Craig twisted the dial again. Brackenridge was playing somebody. He knew *that* name. Then Rawley's voice was back.

"Basically, what it is, Carl, is it comes down to this. Most teams, when they play the pass, they do one of two things. They rush seven men and drop four, or else they come with four and drop off the seven to cover. McKean, shoot, they ain't even playing the pass at *all*. They're putting eight men around that line of scrimmage and they're coming hard every play. They're counting on three defensive backs to play White, Krieg and Duvall head up, flat out man for man, put pressure on the passer, and so far it's worked slicker than a whoopee cushion."

"That's exactly right, Gabby, and like I always say, you have to have field position. You can't spend all night in the shadow of your own goal line. These Owls are going to have to reach back inside themselves and dig out a new platitude of achievement if—"

Again the static broke in. Sound waves seemed to twist somewhere in the air between McKean and the Warren kitchen. "Coal Creek over the ball now. Strong to the right. The ball given off to Dombrowski, the big fullback, piling off tackle." The voice rose to a shriek. "*Fumble!* The ball is loose! We'll have it for you as they unpile. Brackenridge has recovered! Brackenridge has the ball, and for the moment at least the Miners' drive has been stopped at the Brackenridge eleven yard line!"

Coal Creek! Craig sat up a little straighter. The Miners were one of the top teams in the state every year, and this was supposed to be their best team ever. Ranked number one in the *Journal* this morning. And Brackenridge was number three. This might be some game! He fiddled with the knob again, this time trying to make the announcer from Brackenridge slide in around Carmen and Rawley's nonsense.

"So the Bison now with the ball, less than two minutes to go in the game, trailing by a point at fifteen to fourteen, eighty-nine yards away from paydirt. Michelonis, the marked man tonight, only eighty-seven yards on the ground, fifty or so in the air. Still, he's managed a touchdown and two extra points. He has the ball, slams into the right tackle hole, squirms forward to about the eighteen yard line. The clock continues to run."

"What's the score?" Craig's mother asked, entering the kitchen.

Fifteen to fourteen," Craig said.

"Favor of Oiltown?" she asked.

Craig flushed. "This is Coal Creek and Brackenridge, the Miners and the Bison, with Coal Creek on top."

"Oh," said his mother, and went out again.

Craig sighed and twisted the dial again. Carl Carmen's nasal voice was loud and clear. "And here's Gold's field goal attempt! The kick is up. It's long enough! It's straight enough! No good!" Craig hooted. "And so," Carmen continued, "with seconds left to go in the third period, Gold's kick is apparently blown off to the left by these strong cross-field winds we're experiencing here in McKean this evening. The score remains the Owls nothing and the McKean High School Wolves—nothing."

Enough of Carl Carmen, Craig thought. Besides, he wanted to see if the great Michelonis was the miracle worker the papers kept making him out to be.

"Michelonis running wide to the right. Coal Creek strings out the play well, hems him against the sideline —Ooooh, what a hit on Michelonis by Albrecht and Daley! Mike is out of bounds, short of the first down, and he's not getting up. Time is out on the play with about a minute and fifteen seconds left to go in the game."

Craig found himself with his fingers crossed. He was breathing hard.

"That's the way it's gone all night," the announcer was saying. "What a pounding Michelonis has taken from these Miners and how he's kept coming back and back for more. That one hundred seventy-five pounds of his has

73

been thrown at the Coal Creek defensive wall almost twenty-five times tonight, and every time he goes down, you think it's for keeps. That cheer you hear in the background—he's on his feet and in the huddle again. The Bison face third and about a yard on their own twenty."

Craig's father, wearing his green checkered hunting jacket over his work clothes, came in the back door. "Well, bub," he had said earlier, "if you don't have the attitude that says you want to go to McKean, I might as well pick me up some overtime down in the barrel house." Now he grinned at Craig, his annoyance forgotten. "How do you like that score, bub?" he asked.

Craig shushed him, waving both hands. The announcer's voice rose sharply. "Here we go. It's a long count. Michelonis *again* hits straight ahead. *Nothing* there! Hold on. He bounces off the pile. He's running hard to his left. Oh, what a move on Albrecht! He's turned the corner! He's got the first down! He's free at the thirty, still going, across midfield now! Michelonis cuts back. He's hit at the Coal Creek forty! Still on his feet, *refusing* to go down! He's inside the twenty-five. *Listen* to this crowd! Finally they run him down from behind at the Coal Creek thirteen yard line!"

Craig was up with the crowd, shouting "All the way! All the way! All the way!" and when Michelonis went down, he found himself pounding the kitchen table in frustration.

"What's up?" said his father. "All the way, *who?*"

"Mike Michelonis, the guy from Brackenridge."

"Yeah?" Craig's father sat down. "Who they playing?"

"Coal Creek. *Listen* to this!"

"The Bison lining up for the field goal. Thornton will hold. Michelonis backs off his step and a half. It'll be a thirty yarder if he makes it. He's the calmest man in the place. Here's the snap. The ball is down. The kick is on the way. It is . . ."

Then the crowd roar drowned out everything and Craig Warren was pounding his father on the back. "He did it! He did it!"

His father grinned. "Take it easy, bub. Easy. Now all you got to do is beat Brackenridge, eh? Put those Owls right up there at number one."

"I never thought of that," Craig admitted. "I just kind of like that Michelonis. He's—different, you know? You almost expect miracles or something."

"Well, don't like him *too* much. The Owls will put a stop to *him*." His father's face darkened. "Have to do better than tonight, though. Shoot, they were lucky!"

He'd all but forgotten the Owls. "What happened?"

"You don't know?" His father was incredulous. "Finally got a pass interference call. Put the ball on the one yard line. Zale knocked it in. Won, six to zip."

"I hadn't heard," Craig said.

"Tell the truth now, Eagle," said Willie White, "did that little wolfman guy really interfere with you like those zebras said?"

The two boys were leaning against the auditorium doors in the large entrance hall of Oiltown High School. Enormous trophy cases glittered dully along either wall, and as always the students wandered past, some of them stopping long enough to say hello or to stand for a moment or two and talk football. Outside it was foggy, and the yellow leaves of the trees across the street fluttered like barely visible flags. Blue Monday. Ten minutes before the first class of the week.

Not even Mondays could suppress Eagle Duvall. "Well

75

now," he said to Willie White, "I'm not saying he *didn't*. He was *trying* to interfere with the Eagle, don't you know, climbing my back and flapping his little hands against my ear holes, the ones in my football hat. Like I say, he was *trying* to interfere, but, shoot, he wasn't hardly any *bother*. Nothing to keep the Eagle from making a catch."

"Why didn't you catch it, then?" asked a band member who had stopped to listen.

Eagle eyed the saxophone player dourly. "Why didn't I catch it?" Duvall turned to Willie White as if to ask if White knew this stranger. Craig Warren moved in closer. He wanted to know more about the play that had finally beaten McKean. "Why didn't I catch it? Gold threw the doggone ball so far over my head, I was afraid it might end up in the Ladies' Room along aisle B. Kept me from, you might say, *pursuing* the matter."

Clint Gold, who was passing through the entrance hall, overheard, as he was meant to, and reddened. He lowered his head and kept going. Willie White slapped his thigh. "And that was his *good* pass," he cackled as the bell rang.

That afternoon Craig sat in Mr. Craft's room, watching the sun filter a long way down through the trees on the hills outside. This time of year the light was amber, had a kind of thickness almost, something you could taste and smell. Maybe Oiltown didn't look like much, Craig thought, but it was sure situated in an awful pretty place.

Mr. Craft seemed a little distracted these past few days, like his mind was half someplace else, but even with that Craig had to admit he *liked* this class. Mr. Craft could be really interesting, even talking about poetry, and somehow in his room the other kids, especially the bright ones like Dale Davis, said things—serious things—that were

76

different from talk you heard anywhere else in Oiltown. Sometimes Craig had to work really hard to keep himself from jumping into some of the discussions Craft got going, but Zale's scornful presence in the rear of the room kept him slumped in his seat and staring out the window. Craig was listening, all right. But things were tough enough with football, with Zale, without that Artsy-Craftsy routine.

Still Craig had to admit, if only to himself, this was his favorite hour of the day. He was even interested in the things Mr. Craft always had on the board. Every day he wrote out a different quotation in his careful hand that was almost like artwork or something. Sometimes the quotes were funny, and sometimes they set you to thinking a long time. They were what Craft had instead of the slogans Muldoon plastered around the locker room: WHERE THERE'S A BLOCK, THERE'S A WAY! or NO GUTS, NO GLORY! You didn't have to think about those long. They just hit you, as Carl Carmen would say, "right between the nose." But this one of Mr. Craft's today, it was hitting Craig between the nose, too.

"Imagination, imagination, imagination," it read. *"It converts to actual! It sustains, it alters, it redeems . . . ! What Homo sapiens imagines, he may slowly convert himself to."*

Underneath Mr. Craft had written the author's name: Saul Bellow.

Well, that was all right for Saul Bellow, whoever he was, but imagination was the curse of Craig Warren. If there was one thing he had, it was imagination. He could imagine interceptions, fumbles, bumbles of all kinds. He could imagine Clint Gold's driving knees and Eagle Duvall's famous forearm. He could imagine Tiny Daugherty falling ten stories out some window on him.

And he could imagine Coach Muldoon there, scraping him out from under Daugherty and saying, "Warren, we're going to do this until you do it right!" Imagination had never sustained Craig Warren. Or redeemed him, either. What was it Waldo had said? "You think too much." Anyway, who had this Saul Bellow guy ever played for? Nonetheless he found himself copying the quotation carefully in his notebook. Maybe it would be on a test. You never knew.

ELEVEN

Muldoon, Buckwalter and Dykstra were having a high-level strategy meeting, complete with sandwiches and coffee, in the coaches' cramped locker room.

Dykstra looked worried. "Well," he said, "it won't hurt us to slip a little in the state rankings. Maybe some of the helmets will go on easier this week."

"Clint Gold's sure will," said Buckwalter.

"Shoot," said Dykstra, "if we can just get by these next two, three games, we can be playing Brackenridge for all the marbles."

Muldoon said nothing, staring thoughtfully into his coffee cup.

"That won't be any bowl of bagels," said Buckwalter. "That doggone Michelonis has beat us three years running. Remember, Coach?" He nodded toward Muldoon. "Even his freshman year. You weren't here, Gene, but all they used him for was punt returns and kickoff returns. A freshman. We thought we could pick on him, so we kicked away from their other return man."

"What happened?"

"Two touchdowns is what happened. Beat us fourteen to ten, and we were loaded that year. And it's what's *been* happening ever since to darn near every team in the state. That Michelonis, he's something else!"

"Where will he go next year?" Gene Dykstra asked.

Muldoon spoke for the first time. "West Point wants him bad. Most of the Ivy schools, Princeton, Yale, Brown. He's a good student, Michelonis, darn near perfect grades, they tell me."

Dykstra grinned. "Must be *something* he can't do. What about Penn State? Pitt? The Big Ten schools?"

"There are lots of things he can't do," Muldoon said. "He can't run the forty in much under four-nine, for one thing." Buckwalter looked surprised. "And he can't make himself more than six feet, one-seventy-five, either," Muldoon went on. "Those big-time schools, the coaches, they know the numbers. They measure Michelonis and he doesn't measure up. But they can't measure the heart. Or the head."

"You think he could play big time, then?" asked Buckwalter.

"I think I'm glad we don't have to worry about him this week," said Muldoon. "And I think we better make some plans, put in a few things, for this Allenville outfit we play *this* week, this Friday night."

"Allenville's like us," said Dykstra. "They'll look at the films, see what McKean did to us. Cut off the run, and the pass attack commits suicide. What can you do?"

"I can work more with Gold," said Buckwalter. "Trouble is, I've *been* working with Clint since August. He's just not a passer, I'm afraid."

"What about Craig Warren?" asked Dykstra. "You're always saying he's the best pure passer you've ever coached."

"Warren? He's at least a year away. I'm not sure he'll ever be there, to tell you the truth. He's a good thrower, but he doesn't really want to play football."

"It's not next year or this year with him," said Muldoon. "It's all inside, and it could happen tomorrow or never. But we can't count on him for Allenville. Maybe if we get a lead, we'll give him a look."

"How are we going to get a lead?" asked Dykstra. "Allenville isn't stupid. They'll have us scouted, see Gold can't throw a lick, and stack us up same as McKean did."

"Half-smart's as good as stupid," said Muldoon around a mouthful of sandwich. "In this coaching game, you adapt or you lose." He moved quickly to the chalkboard. His wiry hair bobbed as he scribbled X's and O's vigorously across the board. Then he wheeled to face his two assistants. "Well?" he asked, smiling thinly.

Dykstra whistled softly. "I think that's the ticket, coach."

"Muldoon," Buckwalter laughed, "we're going to be as screwy as City Prep with that kind of stuff."

"I know." Muldoon's grin was gone. "I don't like it. You can't build on it. But it will get us by Allenville." He took off his glasses, polished them on his sweatsuit front. "It better."

Craig Warren sat on the bench and watched the Allenville game swirl in front of him. More and more he felt like the action was on television, or in some movie. The crowd noise from behind him seemed muted and distant, as if it were coming through speakers in the back of an enormous theater. It didn't seem real, any of it, and he caught himself expecting spectacular plays to be rerun in slow motion, even found himself missing Carl Carmen's nasal distortions of the play-by-play. He had to admit it was a colorful performance, a vividly choreo-graphed dance in shades of scarlet and white. Allenville looked plenty sharp. The Aviators were decked out in scarlet jerseys with white trim and white pants with a broad scarlet stripe. The helmets were white with a big red A on both sides. Whatever show it was, at least the picture was coming in bright and clear.

Allenville had the Owls in trouble. This was a big game for them, a chance to knock off one of the state's top teams, and they were confident that they had the strategy for success. Their freshman coach had traveled to McKean the week before, and he had watched the undermanned Wolves stop Oiltown cold by daring them to pass. He had made his report, and the Aviators were stacking eight and nine men along the line of scrimmage. It was a fine game plan, and Allenville had the horses to make it work.

On the other hand, the scarlet-jerseyed visitors hadn't devised a way to get around or over or through the Owl defense. Eagle Duvall was a raging maniac, spending most of the first half sitting on top of the Allenville quarterback, and the rest of the black-and-white defend-ers weren't far behind him. The game settled into an uneasy exchange of punts, and Allenville had one of the top punters in the state. They were content to wait for a break.

But when the break came, it wasn't exactly what the Aviator coach had in mind. Midway through the second quarter, the Owls punted from their own 35. The Allenville safetyman charged Gold's short, wobbly kick with the next morning's headlines dancing before his eyes: AVIATORS WIN ON 70 YARD KICK RETURN. A second later the only things dancing in front of his eyes were stars. The ball, the safety man, and Paul Pulaski and

Eagle Duvall all arrived full steam at the same place in the same instant. When the scramble was over, the Owls had the ball on the Allenville 30 yard line.

"There it is," said Muldoon, hunching forward. "That's what we've been needing." He signaled for a time-out, and Clint Gold jogged over to the sideline and bent close while Muldoon talked and gestured quickly. The Owl bench knew what to expect. They'd been working in closed practices all week, and this was the first test of what they'd learned.

The first play was old stuff. The Owls lined up strong left and Gold simply took the ball and pitched back to Zale running wide to the strong side. DeSales led the play and the guards pulled to help out, but there was a stone wall of scarlet waiting for Zale and he went down hard after gaining only a yard.

"Did you see that?" said Muldoon. "Will you look at who made that tackle! Safety man and cornerback. Look at those bozos cheat up!"

The Owls broke the huddle again, this time lining up strong to the right. The home crowd was beginning to get impatient. They had had enough of this sweep, plunge, sweep and punt offense. Once again, Gold took the snap and turned and pitched back to Zale who headed around the right end. Duvall blocked down on the Allenville tackle, but it didn't stick, and the tackle might have smeared Zale for a big loss if Clint Gold hadn't chopped him down with a crossbody block. The Allenville defensive backs were charging hard, trying to force the play before Zale could get turned upfield. Then the Owl back pulled up short. "Pass!" came the shout from the Aviator bench, but it was too late. Zale wasn't a good passer, but the wobbly ball he threw landed in Eagle Duvall's hands like a wounded duck coming down thankfully to its home pond. Duvall had slipped his block and ducked in behind the onrushing Allenville backs and when he caught the pass he was home free. "Just like being on Main Street at two o'clock in the morning," he would tell Muldoon later. Then he noticed his coach's look and added, "Uh, at least that's what I suppose it'd be like."

Gold kicked the extra point and Oiltown led, 7–0. Muldoon was dancing on the sideline. "That'll loosen 'em up!" he chortled. "Teach 'em to fool with a Muldoon team!"

Allenville came right back, marching down the field on a precise series of wishbone plunges and pitches. They ran away from Eagle Duvall on every play, picked on the weaker Owls whenever possible, mixed in an occasional pass. Inside the Owl 30 they were penalized when one of their guards rocked forward just before the ball was snapped, and Steve Bates reacted like a runaway rocket before the guilty Aviator could reset himself. Three running plays and an incomplete pass later, Allenville was short of the first down by less than the length of the football, and the Owls took over deep in their own territory.

Again Gold came to the sideline and conferred with Muldoon. The Aviators were a little uneasy. Their coach paced the sidelines, chewing on a rolled-up program. But the first play was back to basics for the Owls. Zale led DeSales into the off-tackle hole on the left side and the smallish fullback fought his way for three yards before the defensive backs came up to help the linebackers make the stop. Second and seven. "Now's the time," said Muldoon. Craig had never seen him so nervous. Muldoon's eyes were glued to the action and he charged up and down the sidelines recklessly so that players and assistant coaches alike had to be careful not to get run over. "Like a sprinter reading the paper," said Buckwalter to Dykstra.

The next play looked like a carbon copy of the first. "It better," Muldoon had told them a hundred times in practice. Gold took the ball and put it in DeSales's belly as he cracked off tackle to the left. But this time Gold slipped the ball out again and slid it to Eagle Duvall coming back around from the left end slot where he'd lined up. Duvall started running to his right as each of the Owl linemen adjusted by blocking the man who would ordinarily be the assignment of the Owl on his right. Gold chopped down the end who had lined up opposite Duvall. The Allenville safety wasn't completely fooled. "Reverse!" he shouted, and the scarlet Aviators reacted quickly. Nobody wanted to see Eagle Duvall turning the corner and getting up running speed. Suddenly Duvall planted his feet and looked downfield. Eagle Duvall had always loved to throw things. In the spring he threw the discus and the javelin for the track team, and he had school records in both. Now he went through a shortened version of his javelin-throwing technique and uncorked a heave that brought the Owl fans out of their seats in disbelief. Eagle cut loose from his own 25 yard line and the ball shot out like a capsule in orbit. Nobody in the stadium had ever seen a ball thrown farther. Downfield, Willie White was churning for his life, and the ball seemed hopelessly overthrown. But White and Duvall had stayed for a half-hour after every practice working on this one play, and the Eagle knew what White could do. The ball hung and hung in the night air and the crowd howled as White pulled it in only a stride shy of the end zone. He took it in, leaped high, and spiked the ball down over the crossbar of the goalpost. Touchdown!

On the far sideline the Allenville coach slammed his chewed program to the ground in disbelief. "Gol-*dang*-it!" he exploded to his sheepish freshman coach. "Didn't you swear up and down to me they couldn't *throw?*"

"All I said, Coach, was the *quarterback* couldn't throw."

The Allenville coach made a sound deep in his throat, then picked up his program and started chewing again.

The second half was easy. Allenville no longer trusted the defense that had worked for them earlier, and their normal formations were no match for the white-shirted Owls. Oiltown scored on a long drive the first time it had the ball, and then scored again after Mark Thomas recovered an Aviator fumble on the ensuing kickoff. Early in the fourth quarter Eagle Duvall broke through a blocker to bat a pass up in the air. It came down in the pudgy hands of Tiny Daugherty. Daugherty looked bemused momentarily, then began rolling toward the Allenville end zone. Daugherty ran like a berserk rhino, a very old berserk rhino. By the time he finally crossed the goal line, the Owl bench was in an uproar.

"I thought time was going to run out," Buckwalter announced, tears running down his cheeks. With the score 34–0 in favor of Oiltown, Muldoon took mercy and started sending in the reserves. Waldo Frampton was among the first to go in. Waldo had become a far more disciplined player since his transformation two weeks earlier, but he was still applying the principle of physics that had made him notorious on the practice field. Muldoon loved it!

Late in the game, Buckwalter and Muldoon put their heads together. "Good idea, Bill," said Muldoon. He shot a glance along the bench. "Warren!" he snapped. Craig was startled. For a moment he wasn't sure any of this was real.

Muldoon took him by the arm. His bony fingers bit into Craig's biceps. It was real, all right. "Now listen," said Muldoon. "We've got a big lead. There's no pressure. We want to work on our passing game a little. Go in there when we get the ball and put it in the air. No interceptions, now. If nobody's open, put it out of bounds. You got it?" There was a roar of joy from the crowd as the Owl reserves forced an Allenville fumble. Waldo Frampton came out of the pile holding the ball high over his head. "Okay," said Muldoon. "Get out there. Show us what you can do!"

TWELVE

He felt like a man in a diving suit a mile undersea where the pressure of the water made every motion nightmarishly slow. The Owl reserves were huddled and waiting for him, but their faces seemed far off, the whole scene like something seen through the wrong end of a telescope. Then Waldo Frampton whacked him on the shoulder pads and gave him a wink. "Attaboy, Craig! The old momentum! We'll kill 'em! Just kill 'em!"

"Muldoon says to pass," Craig said apologetically, looking around to see who his receivers might be. Arnie Watts at one end, Clyde Thornhill at the other. Not bad. Both looked scared, though. "All right," Craig said, trying to keep his voice steady. "Y right, E flex, flood right. On two!"

"Not so loud," said the substitute center as the Owls broke the huddle.

"On two, on two," chanted the Allenville tackles.

"Great," thought Craig. "Just what I need." Then he began the count. "Down. Black thirty-five. Black thirty-five. Hut—hut!"

He dropped back, hurrying away from the growls and slamming of pads and helmets as the lines came together. Seven yards back he set up, looked out to the right where Watts should be running deep along the sideline and Thornhill should be crossing for a shorter pass. Nothing was there but backpedaling Aviators in scarlet shirts. Craig glanced anxiously to his left. Watts had run the wrong pattern, and he and poor Thornhill had collided and knocked each other silly somewhere over the middle. And now the Allenville linemen had thrown off their blockers and were bearing down on him.

The biggest Aviator was a headhunter. He tried to knock Craig's helmet off with his tackle, and the young quarterback ducked just in time, spun around, and started running like a man leaving a burning building. The rush of the scarlet-and-white line was violent and intense, but the linemen had left a small seam in the middle, and Craig shot through it. Without quite knowing how he got there, he found himself in the center of a huge piece of open territory, with the Aviator backs dropping away in front of him and the linemen's momentum carrying them away in the opposite direction. The crowd din rose to a steady scream. Craig had never expected this. He was running in pure panic, thinking "Now you're REALLY going to get it!" Suddenly there was a thud from his blindside, almost like walking into a wall in the dark, and he and an Allenville linebacker landed together on the soft grass of the field.

A voice somewhere far above them in the night sky announced, "Craig Warren the ballcarrier. Tackle by Santos. A pickup of fifteen on the play." The young Owls were elated. Waldo Frampton pulled Craig to his feet and whacked him on the back. "Way to run, *Craig!*"

Craig was numb. Like everything else in a dream,

getting hit didn't seem real. It hadn't hurt at all. In fact, it was fun, like kids tumbling down a grassy hill or doing rolls in gym class on a thick mat.

"Sorry, Craig," said Arnie Watts. "I messed up."

"It's okay, Arnie," Craig said. For the first time he felt as if the cobwebs were knocked out. Things were in focus again. He knelt in the huddle and called another pass. "You got it, Arnie? Clyde? Watts and Thornhill nodded. This time Craig remembered to keep his voice down when he gave the snap count.

Once again he dropped back, but this time he felt more at home, the way he sometimes felt in the backyard when his receiver was the tire hanging from the old rope. Watts and Thornhill were crossing deep, which should have been no problem for the Allenville backs, but by now the red shirts were mostly filled with reserves, and Thornhill was left absolutely uncovered as he chugged awkwardly across the field. Craig whipped his arm through and watched the ball go. It was beautiful, the lights glinting on the white stripes at either end, the laces turning in a tight spiral, as it landed squarely in Thornhill's hands and then popped out again. The crowd groaned. Thornhill slammed his hands against the sides of his helmet in disbelief.

Muldoon sent in the next play, sending the reserve fullback out of the backfield and up along the sideline while the ends decoyed the defensive backs to the other side of the field. Craig dropped into the pocket, feeling the pressure building from both sides, but when he looked for the fullback he saw the Owl had his man beaten and was churning along on his thick legs and waving for the ball. This time Craig didn't get to watch his work. Just as he released the ball, a beefy Allenville tackle slammed into his ribs and drove him down hard, brought him back to earth with a thud. For a moment, Craig couldn't get his breath. He never saw the ball nose down perfectly into the fullback's hands, never saw his stubby receiver juggle it momentarily and then lose it out of bounds.

"Welcome to football, sucker," said the Allenville player, his face mask close to Craig's ear.

"That's it, gentlemen," said the referee, waving his arms. "That's the game."

Home. No place like it. Craig pushed open the door. His father was standing over the furnace grating between the living and the old high-ceilinged dining room, rubbing his hands together against the chill.

"All right, bub!" he said. "All right! That's more like it, eh?"

Craig had hardly ever seen his father more excited. He grinned. "Yeah," he said. "Those coaches at Penn State are gonna see that oh-for-two in the papers and beat a path to our door, Pop. You'll have to get us an unlisted phone number to keep the recruiters from re*cruit*ing us to death."

His father dismissed Craig's flippancy with an airy wave. "Never mind that. Never mind the balls were dropped. I told 'em. I told 'em in the barrel house, 'You want to see some passing, wait till my boy gets a chance to show what he can do!' Next time you'll have some *receivers* in there, it'll be different!"

Craig's mother came in from the kitchen carrying a plate of cookies. "I thought you might be hungry, dear," she said. She winked at Craig. "Your father's too old to be playing this football. When you made that run, I thought he was going to pound poor Mr. Daugherty to death. I don't imagine the Daughertys will sit in front of us again."

Mr. Warren grinned. "Well, Edna, it isn't every day a

91

man's son plays his first game in Owl Stadium. I felt real strange, real proud. We used to go to those games, remember? Then wear out this old rug replaying them right here in this room. A long time ago."

"Yes," said Mrs. Warren. "We could use a new rug."

"You goin' up to bed already, bub?"

"Yeah. Thanks for the cookies, Mom. I'm kind of tired."

"Imagine it," his father said. "Just imagine it. Two touchdown passes. You could have had two passes for TDs tonight."

"I can't," said Craig.

His father looked puzzled. "What's that? Can't what?"

"I can't imagine it."

"Good night, Craig," said his mother. "*I'd* imagine it would hurt to have all those big people landing on you the way they do."

"Naw," said his father, "I keep telling you, that doesn't hurt. That's football!"

Mr. Warren moved from the floor furnace grate then and sank into the reclining chair that had been "his" for almost as many years as Craig had been alive. Suddenly he looked ten years older than the man who had greeted his only son with such excitement only a few minutes earlier. Older, his wife noted, and not especially healthy.

"Something's missing there, Edna," he said. "He screws up—like down at Fort Steel—he plays real good like tonight—it's all the same to him."

"Don't worry about it so much, Carl," said Mrs. Warren. "You said yourself he did well tonight. That should be enough."

Mr. Warren sat slumped, his head resting in his hands.

"It isn't tonight, Edna," he said very slowly. "There's something—there's something missing in that boy. Call it gumption, call it drive, call it good old-fashioned *guts*."

"Oh, Carl," she said. "Life isn't all football. He's a *good* boy, good in school, never given us the kinds of troubles that so many boys his age—"

"Might have been better if he had," said Carl Warren, lifting his head from his hands and looking directly at his wife. "Those kids—those kids—they aren't *afraid* to make mistakes. They get tough in a hurry or—" He broke off and shrugged.

Mrs. Warren sat silently, watching the pain on her husband's face. Behind him, wind beat against the thin wall of the frame house. Once you moved from the furnace gridwork, it was always cold, fall or winter.

After a long pause, he began again, haltingly, in a muffled voice. "There was a time—I admit it—I thought it was *you*. All those books, hating football the way you do."

Mrs. Warren waited it out.

Then Carl Warren went on. "But I see it more clear now—guts, teaching a kid to fight, that life's a battle, not to give a single inch—that's—that's *father's* work. You've done your part—and more."

Mrs. Warren shifted slightly in her chair, saying nothing, still studying her husband's lined face.

Mr. Warren began again, almost like a man speaking in a trance. "I grew up in this town. We were so poor. I was oldest. Didn't even get the hand-me-downs. Just whatever the old man could scrounge, I guess. Can you imagine how bad I wanted to be *somebody?* Like I say, I grew up in this town. To be a football player—now that was *somebody*."

He broke off, embarrassed. "Hell, Edna," he said sadly. "You've had to listen to this same tune a hundred times before."

Mrs. Warren smiled faintly at her husband. "Carl," she said softly, "there are just some stories—everyone has one—that he *has* to keep telling. Then one day he finally gets it right, and he understands it for the first time." She laughed. "By that time, he's probably seventy and it's too late, but at least he'll have that much—having it right."

"Saint Edna," said Mr. Warren fondly. "One more time then. Like I say, I wanted to be somebody, ratty clothes, whatever.

"What else was I going to do, Edna? I wasn't good with books. You know that. Didn't even know the *names* of the 'right crowd.' Hell, the kids I grew up with, I don't think any of us ever held a football—a *real* football—in our hands. Who had the money for *toys?*"

Mr. Warren slumped in the recliner again as if suddenly very tired. His voice blended with the wind blowing against the walls of the house. Mrs. Warren was listening —for what, she wasn't quite sure. Some change, perhaps, any deviation in the familiar tale.

"I weighed maybe a hundred and thirty pounds, Edna. I didn't even know how to put on the padding. They laughed at me. First day of practice they broke my nose. The old coach—Booke, I think his name was—thought it was funny. 'Warren,' he said to me, 'why not try cross-country or yell-leading?' "

"Maybe you should have tried the cross-country, Carl," said Mrs. Warren. "You might have been really good. You've always had such—endurance."

Mr. Warren waved her off. "Naw, I still would have been nobody. Cross-country those days was just a bunch of crazy freaks in shorts. Who cared what they did?"

He paused a long time, then went on. " 'Sides, that was the fall Mother started to fail—I mean so we all knew. Left my dad and me with the three young brothers to do for. So I dropped out, caught on at the refinery. Been there ever since."

He grinned painfully. "Always will be, I guess—die or retire, one way or the other."

"It hasn't been so bad, has it?" Mrs. Warren asked. "You've always said how much you enjoy the men you work with. And it *is* a job. We've never gone hungry."

"The refinery's been all right," Carl Warren said. "A living. But when *he* was born," nodding his head upstairs, "I made myself one promise. Craig would never end up there."

Mrs. Warren nodded.

"The day he was born, remember, I brought a football, a *real* one, to the hospital. His first present."

Mrs. Warren laughed. "I remember. Some of those old nurses still remember you as the nuttiest new father in a long, long line of nutty fathers."

Mr. Warren was on his feet again, trying to warm himself once more over the old furnace grating.

"And then, remember, from the time he was three, four years old, I took him to every Owl home game. So he could *see* it, see what it might be like to *be* somebody. I admit it. I had dreams—the kid has everything I didn't: size, all the equipment you could want, a real talented arm. I wanted it all for him—to *be* somebody, maybe even a scholarship to some fancy decent college or other."

Mrs. Warren stiffened in her chair. "He'll have *that*," she said. "No matter what or how, he'll have *that!*"

Mr. Warren went on, like a man talking to himself. "But what could I do, Edna? I didn't know anything myself, couldn't, you know, *coach* him like that Zale kid's old man. All I could do was what I did. Show him what it *could* be like, get you to bring home all those dumb books from the library on how to play the game. As if you could learn it from a *book!* And I drove him, tried to, anyway, to practice on his own." He laughed bitterly. "But, like I say, something's missing. That broken nose—"

Mrs. Warren broke in softly. "Oh, Carl," she said, "that nose healed thirty years ago. And the terrible clothes. And your mother's dead almost as long. And you got your brothers through high school—helped, anyway."

Mr. Warren went on staring straight ahead, still rubbing his hands against the cold.

"Craig *will* go to college," she said again fiercely. "There *are* other kinds of scholarships—not just football. He's a good student; he tests well. He can work for some parts of it. And we can cut back some. I've made a list already."

Mr. Warren looked stunned. "Edna, I darn sure don't know where."

Mrs. Warren ignored him. "Craig will have his chance to be 'somebody,'" she said, "if that's how you still want to say it after all these years."

Rising a bit stiffly from her chair, she added, "Time for bed for us old folks." She linked her arm through his. "What I just hope you see *one* time when you tell that story is that doing those things you had to do, you *were* somebody, those thirty years ago.

"And," she added, leading him toward the stairs, "you still are. You always will be."

Craig was being chased by an immense, shadowy figure in an ancient football uniform, a slow-moving hulk like the Frankenstein monster in a horror movie, or like the zombies late-night on TV. He could outrun the monster easily, but there was nowhere to hide, and the thing was tireless. It knocked down doors, appeared suddenly at the ends of hallways, came out from behind curtains. There was nothing behind the face mask but a dark cavern where the nose should have been, a cavern and two eyes, white and crazy as the moon. Craig slipped and fell, started to get up, slipped back again. The thing was close, was closer. It was bending over him, its white crazy eyes inhuman and triumphant.

Craig sat up suddenly in bed. There was nothing. It was the same room he had gone to sleep in every night of his life he could remember. The streetlight glowed dimly outside, illuminating the poster of the Pittsburgh Steeler quarterback on the wall next to his closet. The north wind beat against the side of the old house, and the windows creaked and rattled. Everything was all right. Everything was where it belonged. It was only a dream. Only his imagination playing tricks. Still, whatever it was had said something horrible to him at the last, something so clear it was as if the voice were right there inside the room. Closer. Inside his head. What was it?

Then he had it. "Welcome to football," it had said. "Welcome to football, bub!"

THIRTEEN

*B*lue *Monday again, and only second period. Columns*
of students bent over their books studying Spanish idi-
oms, or pretending to.

From her desk at the front of the room, Señorita
Schmidt watched the heavy light of another October try
to penetrate the dusty windows of the familar room.

Almost ten years before, the señorita had been
hired to teach German—her major at the small
teachers' college where she had, senior year, also been
Homecoming Queen. But, as fewer and fewer Oiltown
students annually bothered to keep up the pretense of
taking the "College Prep" track in the curriculum, the
German classes had withered away. Now she taught
Spanish, French—when there was enough interest
—more often English in the Secretarial Science Depart-
ment. She taught them all with a determined German
accent, but nobody seemed to notice—or care.

She studied the class carefully. Eyes down, backs bent,
row after row. Good order. That was how she liked things.
Then she reached silently into her desk drawer, drew out

and opened her compact. Señorita Schmidt ran a practiced finger at an imaginary smudge at the corner of her carefully done lips.

"Still the fairest of them all," she thought, "not that it matters in this Kingdom of Oil Slicks. No Prince to contend for, only the endless round of wearisome dwarfs —Grumpy, Sleepy, and Dopey."

Suddenly she looked up from the tiny mirror and blinked twice. The wedgelike hulk of Eagle Duvall was making its noisy way up an aisle like a man on his last legs—more accurately on his last *leg*. He was grimacing maniacally—balancing himself by rattling desk after desk as he made his painful way toward her. He paused momentarily, supporting himself with a tremulous hand on the shoulder of Sandra Sherman, cheerleader captain, and pretty enough, Señorita Schmidt supposed, if you liked vapid, gum-popping little blondes.

Then, with an enormous lurch, Eagle dragged himself to the Spanish teacher's desk.

"Yes, Señor Duvall?" she said.

"Señorita," Eagle said, "I was wondering if maybe I could be excused from class today? I have—you might have noticed, ma'am—a bit of an injury, nothing serious, understand, though a bit incapacitatin' for the moment; but Coach Muldoon wants me to see Doc Thornbush this morning, get some treatment so's I can take the field against the Bellevue Academy Bruins this weekend."

Señorita Schmidt looked blankly for a moment into Eagle's dazzling smile. "Bellevue Academy," she said. "That's a fine, fine school."

"Sure is, Señorita," said Eagle, "that's why I especially hope to be physically well enough to play against them this Saturday. A lot of cultural exchanges and that after those games. Chance for some *real* conversations in

Español. Some of those Academy guys, ya know, why it's almost as good as a trip to Acapulco or, uh, Mexico City, some place like that."

Señorita Schmidt hesitated. "Shouldn't you have a note from Doctor Thornbush, Mr. Muldoon, someone?"

"Well, yes, ma'am," said Eagle smiling even more broadly, leaning forward as if to impart some confidentiality. "I guess technically—but Coach Muldoon, well, he's awful busy, what with teaching geometry, and the football, and of course making final arrangements with Bellevue's—what do you call it?—headmaster? for the big cultural winging followin' the game."

Craig Warren watched enviously from his desk in the third row. Not even the teachers could resist Eagle Duvall.

Señorita Schmidt found herself smiling back at the hulking young student.

"Well, all right—this one time, Aguila," she said. "Since there is so much educational value involved—but Aguila, this does not excuse you from the homework assignment—or, now that I think of it, from last Friday's, which as I recall, you have yet to turn in. *Verdad?*"

"*Muchas gracias, Señorita,*" said Eagle, lifting the teacher's brightly nailed right hand swiftly to his lips.

For a moment Craig thought that even Eagle had gone too far for once, but then the huge end was in rapid motion back down the aisle, still limping a bit, but traveling at a clip faster than some of the scrub running backs at top speed.

Suddenly Eagle hooked a powerful hand under Craig's arm and yanked him forcefully to his feet. "C'mon, Warren," he said. It was hard to tell who was more amazed—Señorita Schmidt or Craig Warren. Señorita Schmidt regained her power of speech first. "Señor

Duvall," she said, blushing, "I gave *you* permission to go to the doctor. Do you now mean to tell me that Señor Warren is also in need of medical attention?"

"Oh no, ma'am," said Eagle, over his shoulder as he propelled Craig toward the door. "He's my *precaution* you might say, like a chauffeur—get me there and back, just in case I should pass out from pain or something, you understand."

Eagle paused a brief moment in the doorway. "Thanks again, Señorita," he said. Then, with a quick wink to the rest of the class, "*Adios, muchachas.*" And the door slammed behind him.

They were in the parking lot, squinting into the smoke-fall light almost before Craig realized what he was doing. Skipping school, *truancy*—there was no other word for it. Craig Warren was in open territory again. It felt like the scramble against Allenville. Pure panic.

Craig was surprised to see that Eagle still had a trace of a limp, now that the need for an act was over. But now, instead of favoring the leg, he seemed to drive it furiously into the crumbling asphalt of the parking lot.

"*Move* it, Warren," he said, "we haven't got all day."

"Eagle, you go on if you want. I'm not sure this is such a hot idea for me."

But Eagle was booming full speed ahead, his fingers digging sharply into Craig's biceps like needles pumping some sort of high-powered transfusion of blood.

"Here we are," said Eagle, pausing proudly in front of an outrageously painted and much-battered car. "They really knew how to make 'em back then."

Craig eyed the vehicle doubtfully. It had been hand-painted in Owl colors, more or less white, with enormous black "88's" emblazoned on the trunk and hood. A crudely painted eagle graced the one undented door. Maybe it was an owl. Craig couldn't tell. Knowing Eagle, it could have been either one.

"You're a bright guy, Warren," Eagle said. "It's just sometimes you let school interfere *too* much with your education. Now hop in."

Craig looked at the metal sign at the head of the parking space which Eagle's bumper was bending forward. It read: RESERVED. SUPERINTENDENT ONLY. Speechless, Craig pointed to the sign.

"Makes it perfect," said Duvall. "Nobody's even *seen* that guy for years, not counting that same yearbook picture they've been running forever. Doubt if he could find the doggone *school*, let alone his precious parking place."

"Aren't you afraid they'll tow you away?"

"Naw. How would anybody know this *wasn't* the superintendent's car? You think they're crazy enough to tow *him* away? Now, c'mon, Warren, for the last time, get in."

Craig tugged at the misshapen door on the passenger side, found it wouldn't budge.

"Takes a little know-how," said Eagle. He rattled the door inward with a sinewy forearm, then gave the handle a massive yank. The door groaned open. Then Eagle's hand was on Craig's back, and Craig found himself sprawled across the ancient upholstery and broken springs of the Eaglemobile.

Because Eagle said nothing, only hummed to himself as he drove down the hilly streets of Oiltown toward Main Street and swung his white-and-black clunker noisily around the public square, and because Craig had never known what to expect from Duvall, he was completely amazed when Eagle jammed his tires along the curb in front of the Odd Fellows' Building, tallest in town at eight stories. Maybe Eagle really *was* going to see Doc Thornbush, whose dingy office was on the top floor.

Craig turned toward the driver, mouth open, but there was no answer there, only empty space. Eagle was already swinging around the battered hood, wrenching open Craig's door, and urging him out with an impatient gesture.

As they started up the stairs into the musty dark of the office building, a pair of hairy, tattooed arms bearhugged Eagle just above the elbows from behind.

"You wet-behind-the-ears punk," snarled a disguised voice. "Whatcha doin' skippin' school? You wanna end up in jail?"

Eagle shrugged off the burly arms as if they were bits of yarn. Without turning around, he said, "*Clive* Keller, as I live and breathe."

Craig turned and took Keller in. He was a heavyset man with a mean cast to his eyes and mouth. He was trying to smile now. Craig could tell Keller was a man working with facial muscles he didn't use often.

"Aw, Eagle," he whined, "how'd ya know it was me?"

"Not many men alive with a buzzard breath like yours, Clive," said Eagle, turning to face Keller. Eagle wasn't smiling.

"C'mon, Eagle," said Keller. "Not even my mother calls me *that*. The name is 'Quick,' remember?"

"Yeah," said Eagle, "I keep forgetting. By the way, this here's my friend, Craig Warren. Warren, meet Clive Keller. He'd be in Oiltown's Hall of Fame, he claims, if Oiltown *had* a Hall of Fame."

Keller shot Craig the briefest of uninterested glances, then gave Craig's hand a cold, perfunctory pump and turned back immediately to Eagle.

Taking a kind of half-comic gunfighter's stance in front of the building, still trying to sustain a smile, Keller said, "Next time you forget my name, *boy*, you'll find this here town ain't big enough for the both of us."

For the first time, Eagle grinned thinly. Glancing at Keller's pudgy midsection, he drawled, "Heck, Clive, a town this size ought to have a mirror at the end of Main Street just to make it *look* bigger. Ya know, you keep *expandin'* like you been and Oiltown won't be big enough for *you* all by yourself, let alone any of us normal-size people."

"That tears it," said Keller, propping a heavy elbow on one of Duvall's dented fenders. "Get your puny arm up here. I'll arm rassle you for it. Loser's out of Oiltown by sunset. King of the Hill!"

" 'Fraid I'll have to concede this one to you," said Eagle, "Truth is, me 'n Warren here got some business to take care of. Besides, Clive, any man capable of suckin' *that* wind in and out his lungs all these years has got to have a *natural* strength way beyond an ordinary man."

Keller's smile muscles were beginning to give way under the strain.

"You kids today," he said, "you're all soft. Lift a few weights, pump a little iron, starin' in the mirror the whole time like a bunch of sissies, and then prance around and tell each other how pretty you are."

Eagle was smiling broadly now, but as he turned back toward the stairs, Keller went on with increased bitterness. "*May* day," he said, "we didn't have all that junk. Didn't need it. We had *work* is what we had. Up in the morning, still dark, every morning the chores, then walk six miles to school—any weather—then football practice, walk six miles home. Then it was totin' hay bales till dark, splittin' cords a wood, drivin' nails to hold the old house together. Now *that* was the days when football players was *men, strong* men."

"Smart, too," said Eagle, starting up the stairs leading into the shabby office building. "Knew enough to walk the same number of miles comin' as goin'."

Craig watched Keller's face relax into its accustomed hard meanness. The older man crossed the sidewalk, pressed close to Duvall's back. "One more thing," Keller hissed angrily. "We *played* the game. Played it hurt, played it injured, didn't duck out for every teeny bump, bruise and scrape like a bunch of Camp Fire Girls."

Craig couldn't help feeling a little sorry for Quick Keller, but then he saw something dark pass like a quick shadow over Eagle Duvall's face.

Spinning swiftly, Eagle gripped the bulky ex-halfback just above the elbows and, with no change of expression, no sign of effort whatsoever, he lifted Keller a foot off the pavement, carried him casually back across the sidewalk and, biceps swelling hugely, deposited the older man on the lumpy fender of the Eaglemobile.

Keller's jaw dropped open, but Eagle had already spun on his heel and was on his way into the building again.

"Tell you what, Clive," he said over his shoulder just before the heavy door swung shut, "about that arm rassling—like I say, maybe it's safer if I just *concede*, ya know. I mean, all that hay baling and cow milking and nailing and all. I'd most likely end up getting hurt. Be just another one of those Camp Fire Girls of yours."

Doc Thornbush was actually a chiropractor, the only one in the county, who supplemented his meager income by serving as part-time trainer to the Oiltown athletic teams. He was a sour bald little man with a thin fringe of whitish hair stretching from one hairy ear to the other.

"All right, Duvall," he said, "get your star's fanny up on the table. Take that shoe and sock off. Roll up your pant leg."

Feeling out of place and glum, the warning voice still echoing in his head, Craig Warren carefully parted two slats of Doc Thornbush's dusty window blinds and stared out through the greasy window. Across the valley, on the hills to the north, the long slant of October light smoldered on the drab houses and on the few yellow leaves still clinging to the stark trees. Directly below a few cars idly circled the public square with its tiny bandstand, the war memorial with the inscribed names of the dead. Scattered about the almost grassless little park were two or three rusting green benches where a few elderly men seemed to doze under shapeless, old-fashioned hats.

Turning back to Duvall and Thornbush, Craig stared, flabbergasted by what he saw. Doc Thornbush was rubbing some sort of colorless oil on Eagle's left ankle—an ankle almost completely purplish-blue and swollen to twice its normal size. Above the ankle, on the outside of Eagle's diamond-hard calf, an ugly green and yellow bruise was just beginning to fade.

Duvall's shin was laced almost to the knee with a patchwork—cleat scrapings, Craig guessed, some of them old enough to have whitened to memories, most still raw and scabbed over.

With a flourish, Doc Thornbush handed Eagle a microphone-shaped device attached to a long cord.

"Ultrasound," he announced proudly. "Latest thing. Probably not another one like this baby between here and Buffalo. Should fix you right up."

"Ultrasound, eh?" Duvall grinned. "What do I do with this, Doc? Put it in my ear?"

Thornbush couldn't keep his lower lip from pouting a bit. "Put it anywhere you want, Duvall," he said. "Look here, if you don't trust what the best medical technology can do for you, why don't you just soak in the school whirlpool, same as everybody else?"

Eagle chuckled. "You know how it is, Doc. If Duvall's hurt, everybody's hurt. They see me in there and pretty soon all those hypochondriacs will be fighting each other for tub time. Might cause team dissension, you know?"

"That's right, Duvall," said Thornbush, "I keep forgetting you're this year's invincible hero."

"Besides," Eagle went on, ignoring the smaller man, "suppose Tiny Daugherty should take it into his chubby head that *he's* hurt? I mean old Tiny could get stuck in that weeny tin whirlpool and just plumb *wrinkle* himself to death 'fore anybody could get a crane in there to pry him out."

Thornbush wasn't interested. "A treatment a day, Duvall. You've got the whole week. Swelling should be almost gone by Saturday. Then we'll tape it up good, tell Muldoon to let Bellevue have a break, maybe even give the great Eagle Duvall some bench time."

The chiropractor turned to go into the small outer room where he kept his financial records. Thornbush said, "If it was up to me, I'd just shoot that darn ankle full of Novocain before the game. You wouldn't feel a thing. But that rock-head Muldoon goes crazy if I even *mention* that kind of stuff. My hands are tied. So it's ultrasound for a week. Meantime, stay off that leg as much as possible."

Thornbush turned again. With a wink at Craig, Eagle quickly did a more-than-decent quacking duck call into his fist.

Thornbush spun about angrily. "What was that?" he demanded.

"Just a hacking cough, Doc," Eagle said. "Had the doggone thing for *weeks* now."

"Maybe you should do something about it," Thornbush said icily.

"Yeah, I know," said Eagle. "I've been thinking about goin' to see a doctor."

"When the buzzer over there goes off," said Doc Thornbush, "treatment's over. You know the way out." Then he was gone, closing the door firmly behind him.

"Eagle," Craig said, "I never realized. I mean—I guess I just thought you wanted to get out of a Spanish class or something."

Duvall's dark eyes burned furiously into Craig's for a long, frightening time. Craig felt suddenly weak, almost as if he had taken a powerful physical blow.

"Dammit, Warren," Eagle said. "You always seemed smarter than the rest of these bozos. What the hell *did* you think? Eagle Duvall, the Man of Steel? Strange visitor from another planet? Able to leap tall blockers at a single bound? Put a torch to that white eighty-eight jersey and it won't burn? Nothing to it! Shoot! Even machine-gun bullets bounce like rubber off the mighty Duvall. *Supereagle!* Where you been living all these years, Warren? In the freakin' comic books?"

Then Duvall looked down again and began working the ultrasound device furiously up and down his bloated ankle.

FOURTEEN

*B*ack *in the old car, still parked across from the* public square, Eagle sat for a long moment, fingers drumming on his knobbed steering wheel. Craig broke the silence. "Eagle," he asked, "is that why you brought me along? You wanted me to see that?"

"Stow it, Warren," said Eagle impatiently. "I don't want sympathy from you, from anyone. Listen, there isn't *anybody* I'd rather be than Eagle Duvall. And you know why? Because I know all week, every week, Fort Steel or Allenville or McKean, those meathead coaches are singin' the same old song: 'Stop Duvall, stop Duvall, stop Duvall! On offense, don't let him get to the passer. Defense, jam him up at the line so he can't get out there where he can *catch* anything!' " Eagle closed his eyes and smiled. "Every game a new gimmick. Double-team, triple-team, sometimes something fancy where they come after me with a back in motion. And you know what? I *love* it, Warren. It's what juices me up, makes me stronger. It's all for me, see, and I don't want *anybody* to go away feelin' he didn't get every last thing he paid for."

Craig stared out at the bandstand in the square, trying to imagine what it would be like to be an Eagle Duvall. It would be like living in a foreign country, he thought, maybe even in some different galaxy.

He was surprised when Eagle went on. "The best is when they throw some really tough kid at you, like that big animal, Kolo, from Fort Steel—I mean I *really* loved that game. It's the weak ones—the ones who can't beat you any other way—they go to the hold and the clip and then the leg whipping.

"Good old ultrasound," Eagle grinned. "But they still haven't any meathead one of them stopped Duvall." With a glace at his watch, he added, "Enough chit-chat! A little hustle, Warren, and we just got time for a couple quick greaseburgers at Anderson's Diner, still make it back to school for lunch."

"Eagle," Craig said, "I'm not sure I can imagine what you're telling me, even a little. What I for sure don't understand is *why* you're taking time to tell *me* all this. I mean, I don't play, not even in practices much. Heck, I don't even have any *friends* on the team, unless you count maybe Waldo Frampton."

Duvall's grin vanished. Craig looked down at the worn floormats of the old car, then away, out the window at the crumbling bandstand, at the long war memorial.

"Let's just say your case *interests* me, okay?" Duvall said. "You *should've* quit football after Fort Steel. Anybody with half a brain would have. And again after City Prep. Again after McKean. Shoot, even before the season got started. Most times I don't even think you *like* football. But for some crazy reason you're still out there. So call it curiosity. I'm interested in loonies."

So that was all there was to it. Craig's eyes stung for a

moment. It was simple enough. When Craig turned back, he found Eagle's expression had turned suddenly fierce, something like the one opposing players saw on game nights.

"Why and why and why," he snarled. "What's it to you? Look, Warren, this is Eagle Duvall, not the freakin' Salvation Army, get it? *Anything* I do, I do for Duvall, get it?"

"All right, you want a 'why' so bad! I'll level with you. The Eagle hears things. First of this year—Penn State, Pitt, Syracuse, all of 'em—even as a junior, Eagle Duvall was top-of-the-list tight end prospect for this whole state. *These* days what I'm hearin' is 'Duvall's *among* the best.' " Eagle laughed scornfully. "You know who's number one *now*? *Bill Pipp* from Coal Creek! Can you believe it?" Eagle cleared his throat, muscled down his window and spat derisively. "Give anything to play those clowns this year. I'd turn that Pipp into Pippsqueak in about two minutes."

"I don't get it," said Craig. "You've been playing *great*. What happened?"

"Statistics is what happened," Eagle said bitterly. "That's what happened. Old Pippsqueak has that slick lefty passer, Art Lambert, throwing to *him*. I've got Clint Gold. Hell, Pipp has caught more passes just for *touchdowns* alone than I've caught *total* all year. And the season's half over, Warren. I don't know if you're too far gone to even *notice* stuff like that, but it is."

Eagle drummed his long fingers on the steering wheel. Then he went on. "I got this letter the other day, from Ohio State—the Buckeyes—wanted to know if I thought maybe I could convert to tackle. Fit right in with their *system*, they said. Be another Jim Parker, all that stuff."

111

Craig whistled softly. "Lord, Eagle," he said, "that's the big time! Michigan on TV every year. The Rose Bowl! What else is there?"

Eagle Duvall studied his huge, flexible hands. "I know something about what I am, Warren," he said, "and *one* of the things I am is a pass catcher. That is, I'm a pass catcher when I can find me a quarterback who can throw his hat out of a rowboat and hit the ocean. *That's* where you come in, turkey. I've seen how you throw a football. Real pretty. Professional almost. And those were some nice tosses Friday night against Allenville."

Craig made a small, hopeless gesture. "Why even bother with it, Eagle?" he asked. "When I don't get on Muldoon's nerves, I'm lucky to be the last man on the travel team. The City Prep game? I was the only one of us who never got off the bench. Waldo Frampton is a million miles ahead of me. Beat out Clint Gold? What a joke! Shoot, I don't even split playing time with Al Hanson on the stupid scout team."

For the first time, Eagle Duvall looked tired. He let out a long breath, leaned his head against the antique steering wheel, let his nose rest momentarily on the bridge of his thumb and forefinger.

"Look, Warren, I just told you I'm not the Salvation Army. Well, I'm nobody's free shrink, either."

He paused, then lifted his head and turned over the ignition key. After a noisy protest, the old engine sputtered irregularly into life. Without shifting into gear, still staring straight ahead, Duvall said, "My father—he died, you know when I was ten—"

"I know," said Craig. "That must have been—"

Eagle waved him silent with an impatient gesture. "It happens," he said. "Tell you the truth, Warren, I can't even *remember* him so good anymore. Only reason I

112

brought it up just then is sometimes you and the old man remind me of each other—the two *why-ing-est* people I ever met in my life."

Craig misheard. "*Whiningest?*" he asked.

"Naw," Duvall said. "*Whine* is a step up. A Why-er is somebody who has to have a reason for *everything*. And I mean everything. Like, every kid wants a dog, right? So one day I—you might say—*induced* this stray mutt that had been hanging around the park for days, got it to follow me home. There was the old man at the front door. 'Eagle, why would you go bringin' a *dog* home? Stupid animals don't do a thing in the blessed world 'cept eat and bark and be looked after and mess all over your lawn.' So much for the dog."

Eagle shifted into gear, pulled noisily away from the curb. "Pee Wee football? He wouldn't even sign the consent forms. '*Why* would you want to go out there with a bunch of tomfool kids and chase a bag of wind around till you get hurt?' "

Craig looked out again through the cracked passenger window. The old men went on dozing in the autumn sunlight. The Indian summer glimmer changed everything, made it look serene, beautiful, even the sluggish unhealthy-looking pigeons waddling insolently about the sleepers' old-fashioned, high-topped shoes.

As they swung around the square and started down Main Street, Duvall surprised Craig by going on. "One time a couple older friends of my parents dropped in to visit. The lady was real pregnant. Happy about it, too. Soon's they left, what do you think the old man said? You got it! '*Why* would anybody go do a damnfool thing like that at *their* age?' When he died, the doctors had a fancy name for it, but I always just figured he woke up one morning, took the whole question just one little step

113

back, couldn't find a *why* in the whole blue-eyed world made it worth his time."

Then, humming to himself again, Eagle wheeled his white-and-black heap effortlessly through the small-town traffic maze of creeping refinery tankers and double-parked beer trucks.

Craig rubbed his eyes, like a man trying to wake from a long sleep. He tried to see Oiltown, *really* see it, the way it would be for some tourist, just in, just passing through. This was the only Main Street Craig had ever known—not counting a few ballgame trips with his father to the real cities, to Pittsburgh, to Buffalo, even to Cleveland once. Nothing changed much, that was sure: the same rows of drab brick storefronts, many of them boarded over, with tattered THIS SPACE FOR RENT signs flapping in the wind; the Oiltown Bijou still running the same Walt Disney pictures; the same loiterers, men out of work, not much hope of finding any, forever leaning against the same lampposts, forever spending the time. Most of the real shoppers, Craig knew, people with a little money in their pockets and with cars, would be out at the new shopping mall which shimmered like a mirage of asphalt and cinder blocks just outside Oiltown to the north.

He glanced at Duvall, wondering if the Eagle took in any of it at all. For the briefest of moments, Craig had an image of powerful wings circling over Oiltown, of eyes penetrating enough to see it clear and whole, see every intricate angle. Then Duvall stopped humming long enough to jam a forceful elbow into Craig's ribs. "Make you a bet, sucker," he said. "Bet I can work this same death-threatening ankle scam on that sex-crazed señorita every day this week. Loser pays off for all burgers on Friday? What say?"

Craig agreed glumly. He knew he'd lose, end up paying, knew too that Duvall had got it right, back there in Thornbush's office. Craig Warren had been living in the comic books too long.

Eagle cursed softly, brought his car to a lurching stop as the light turned red at the Route 219 intersection. "Brake linings passed inspection courtesy Tony Ramillo's Pennzoil," Eagle grinned. "Likes his football, that Tony."

"Eagle," Craig suddenly blurted, "I know it's not my business, but I can't even imagine what it must *feel* like. I mean the Buckeyes, Penn State, Pittsburgh. All your life you dream about it—playing on TV, the bowl games, maybe even All-American or something. Like I say, that's the big time."

"Let's get one thing straight, buddy," Eagle said, eyeing the light. "You want to talk about the 'big time'? Well, I've *met* the big time now, dozens of 'em, those 'big-time' coaches. A lot of wavy hair and Hollywood smiles and promises. Not a one of 'em doesn't have that old won-lost record written down in ink someplace on his big-time body 'case he should wake up some bad night in a town like this and forget what it is."

Eagle chuckled darkly. "Tell you what's funny about *that*, friend," he said. "Those guys, every big-time one of 'em, thinks *he's* going to use Eagle Duvall. 'Where can we fit this hick into *our* system?' 'Is this *particular* dumb jock a wheel or a cog or a sprocket or a spring or just what?'"

Duvall turned to face Craig, his rugged face suddenly fierce. "Well, I'll tell you how it's going to *be*, Warren. The Eagle is going to use *them*. Oh, they'll get their money's worth. I meant it when I said I love football—but the *game*. The Rose Bowl, Brackenridge High—it's all the same to me."

Eagle's uncharacteristic monologue was cut short by an

angry blaring of horns. Duvall managed to wrestle his car window down just enough to wedge out his head and massive shoulders. He stared casually at the drivers behind him, and the horn-blowers found themselves suddenly fascinated by the alternating times and temperatures flashing scoreboard-style on the sign that topped the Producer's Savings and Loan.

When he had absolute quiet, Duvall wriggled his torso back through the window and stared straight ahead, apparently quite content to wait out the green light. Then Eagle went on, almost inaudibly, "Football's not the *university*, Warren. Shoot, out of all these boneheads around here, you know *that*. I mean, *damn*—a real university—nobody in my family ever—"

Then Eagle broke off, inched his white-and-black clunker through the intersection, and led his small caravan of traffic at a funeral pace down Main Street. He eyed the sorry parade in his blurred rearview mirror without apparent interest, then made his maddeningly slow turn into the lot at Anderson's Diner.

Craig expected Duvall to be in high gear again, already out the door on his way to one of Anderson's renowned greasy burgers. But the big end sat motionless, staring into the bowl of his powerful hands. After a while he glanced warily at Craig Warren, then began talking again, his voice so low that Craig had to strain to hear him.

"I'm no Einstein, friend, but I ain't just your common, garden-variety thump-head, either. A while back there I told you I know some what I am. Never mind that pass-catcher stuff. That's not important—not really. What *is* important is this other 'Eagle' that keeps peckin' and flappin' and beatin' at my gizzard, understand? *It* wants to go somewhere, someplace it already knows it's *supposed* to go. Does that sound crazy?"

116

It didn't. Not to Craig.

Duvall looked directly at him, his voice no longer a whisper. "Just let me get a *toe* in one of those universities —and it won't be bowl games decide which one it'll be—there'll be *something* there. It won't take much. A little stuff at the bottom of some test tube, some microscope; a leftover scrawl on a blackboard; maybe some mumble out of the beard of one of those professors. *He* won't even think it's important most likely." Eagle winced. "Who knows? It might even be in a *book*.

"But I'll tell you this, Craig," he went on, his voice rising, sounding like the old Eagle again, "When I *see* it, I'll know it—then—" he made a talonlike gripping gesture with hooked fingers, "I won't let go until I take it as far as I can, to wherever it is it's supposed to go! And you know what? When it gets tough on the way—and it will—I'll just say 'Why *not*?' and 'Thanks, Dad.'"

Before Craig could say anything, Duvall was back at full speed on his way out of the car. "C'mon, Warren," he said just before the door slammed. "Haul tail. Between all your yakkin' and those rude high-insurance-risk types what held us up back there at the light, we'll be *real* lucky to make it back for lunch."

Craig watched Eagle's broad back disappear into Anderson's, then shrugged. "Why not?" he asked himself aloud. Then he gave the stubborn door a solid kick and was off after his friend.

FIFTEEN

*A*nyone driving the highway north from Pittsburgh to Buffalo would pass through Oiltown. And if he caught the red light at the corner of Main Street, he would have to wonder about the sanity of the cluster of men across the street in front of the rundown building with a faded sign reading "Oiltown Hotel." The wind was cold, almost as if it were getting ready to snow, and there were more leaves blowing down the streets than on the trees. Anybody with any sense would be in a car with the heater on high, headed for a bigger city. Or at least be in one of the bleak stores along Main Street, earning a living or buying a heavy coat. Who were these nuts, anyway? And what had them so excited, all that arm-waving and fist-shaking? Then the light would change, and anyone would shift gears, turn left on Main Street, cross the bridge over the creek with its tin cans and paper bags snagged on rocks, and drive out of town past the smokestacks of the refinery. Soon he would be in the rolling hills to the north, and Oiltown would be forgotten.

"I ain't sayin' Allenville ain't tough. What I'm sayin' is

they ain't tough like in the *old* days! The schedule's soft. Not like ours. Not like who we played!" That was Quick Keller. Most of the men nodded. Nothing was quite the same nowadays. Not the dollar, not even the oilfields. Not these kids with their cars and hair down over their ears. Soft.

"I dunno," said Joe Hugo. "It's the same teams. Brackenridge, Oldfield, Prep. Always the same. McKean."

"Yeah," said Keller. "But like look at this next team we got. Bellevue *Academy*. Not even a real school, for gosh sakes! An *academy*." He spit carefully, going with the strong wind.

"That's right," said Perenchio. "Paper this morning says they haven't won a game this season."

"*This* season!" exploded Keller. "Bellevue hasn't won in fifteen straight! Now you tell me, Joey H, why'd we schedule a team like that?"

"Muldoon's no dummy," said Joe Hugo. "He knows what's coming. After Bellevue he's got Oldfield and Brackenridge back to back. Besides, when he made this schedule out, probably three, four years ago, Bellevue was half decent."

"Well," said Perenchio, "how about Oldfield? They got Brackenridge and *us* back to back and no Bellevue Academy to bail them out. The number one team in the state and—what're we now? Back in the top five."

"Oldfield's in tough," Hugo agreed. "But this Bellevue, now, this game may be a good thing. Give Muldoon a chance to get the passing game going. You can't have your darn linemen throwing the ball seventy yards *every* week. That stuff works once a season."

"That Duvall is something!" said another man. "Throws the ball better than any quarterback."

"Throws it *farther*," said Joe Hugo. "Farther ain't always better. Did you see that windup on Duvall, looked like one of those spear throwers or something. No, Duvall's no quarterback. Tight end's where he'll be in college, tight end's where he should play here."

"How about this other kid?" asked Quick Keller. "This Warren, the backup quarterback? He throws a nice ball."

"Runs good, too," Perenchio said. "Scrambled real well that one time."

"Runs scared," said Joe Hugo, pulling his collar close around his ears and hunching against the cold. "And scared won't get it done."

Bellevue Academy was a handsome scattering of stone buildings with ivied walls. The campus spread out for acres on a forested hilltop that would have done credit to any small college. The Owls were impressed. Their battered bus made its way slowly past the white-steepled chapel, around a tree-lined quadrangle, and pulled up in front of the high arches of the fieldhouse. Johnny Zale whistled, "Fan-cy!"

It was a beautiful Saturday afternoon, the sun blowing fitfully in the yellow maples. It seemed odd to be playing football in daylight, a long way from the refinery towers back home, even a long way from the coal piles and huge smokestacks of a place like Fort Steel. Whatever a football town was, this Bellevue Academy was something else.

When the game began there were only a few fans scattered noiselessly about on the Academy side. The Oiltown rooters who had made the trip were a much rowdier lot, and supremely confident. And the Bellevue team *did* seem snake-bit. Their deep receiver fumbled the opening kickoff, kicked the ball in trying to pick it up, dove on it and watched in horror as it squirted out from under him like a cake of soap in a bathtub. Billy Krieg came up with it, and it took the Owls four plays, including an incomplete pass, to push the ball into the end zone. Zale romped in untouched. The Owl fans whooped it up. The Bellevue side was quiet except for an occasional shout of "Let's go, Bruins."

The Bruins handled the next kickoff satisfactorily, even made a quick first down on a nice pass over the middle to the left end, but the drive bogged down when they were flagged twice consecutively for being offsides.

"Look at that team," said Muldoon sadly. "They don't come off the ball like a football team. It's like a typewriter out there. Clack, clack, clack, one lineman at a time."

"I know it," said Buckwalter. "And look at the backs. One of them back on his heels, one of them leaning left, one of them all white knuckles and weight on the forward arm. You know where they're going every play."

The Owls rolled to two quick first downs, and then Clint Gold threw a wobbly pass to Billy Krieg alone in the end zone. The Bruins had misread the play badly, and two of them were still chasing Eagle Duvall as Krieg spiked the ball after the touchdown.

When it became apparent that the Academy Bruins weren't able to generate any offense, Muldoon had a hurried conference with Dykstra and Buckwalter. "Good idea," he said, nodding his head. "We'll see how that lineup looks." He scanned the bench, fixed an eye on Craig. "Warren," he snapped, "get up here. You ready to play?"

"Yessir. I think so."

Muldoon's face darkened. "You *think* so? Would you like some more time to wrestle with it? You *think* so? What'd you come over here for? You *think* so!"

"No. I mean, I'm ready."

Muldoon muttered under his breath. "All right," he said. "Never mind all that. Go in there for DeSales and have Goldie move to fullback. He's got the plays down. Old home week for Gold. I want you to throw the ball. Got it? I want to see that passing game, want to see the timing with the good receivers in there."

The Bruins punted once again and the ball rolled dead just across midfield in Owl territory. "All right," said Muldoon. "Let's see what you can do."

When he saw Craig trotting out, Gold started for the bench, but Craig grabbed him by the arm. "Coach says you should run fullback," he said. Gold stared for a moment, not taking it in, like news too good to believe. "All *right!*" he sighed. "Back in the saddle. All right!"

Craig ducked in the huddle, looked around at the black-shirted first unit. "Coach says—" he began, but Gold interrupted.

"Fullback thirty-six slant," he said.

"Coach says—"

"Thirty-six slant!"

"Come on," said Eagle Duvall, "run a play."

"Thirty-six slant," Craig said, "on three."

Gold took the handoff and powered his way, bouncing off Bruin tacklers like a brahma bull scattering riders and clowns, and was finally stopped after a gain of a dozen yards.

"Run it again," he said in the huddle.

"Who's quarterback?" said Duvall.

"I am," Craig said.

"Act like it, then," snapped Duvall.

"Thirty-six slant," said Gold. "Come on, Warren. Just call the snap count."

The referee's whistle sounded. Too much time.

"What the devil's going on out there?" glowered Muldoon.

"Looks like an awfully talkative huddle," said Dykstra.

"A debate. That's what's going on there," said Buckwalter.

Again the Owls rolled up to the line, and again the give was to Clint Gold slanting off the right tackle. This time the Bruins met him at the line and stopped him for a gain of four or five.

Waldo Frampton came sprinting across the field and ducked into the huddle. "Muldoon says *pass*," he hissed. "He's awful mad, Craig."

"Okay," said Craig. "Okay. Let's go with a wide right—"

This time it was Zale who broke in. "Halfback pass," he demanded.

"Muldoon said pass."

"Halfback option *is* a pass. Only I'm throwin'! Get out there, Eagle!"

Duvall looked hard at Craig Warren. Then he shrugged elaborately. "Your funeral," he said.

"Halfback option pass," Zale announced. "Run it on *two*. Come on, Artsy-Craftsy, let's get going."

The ball slapped hard into Craig's left hand and he started down the line to his right, trying to make the play look like an option. When he got to the Academy end, he pitched back to Zale, and threw himself at the end's knees. It was a poor block, and he knew it, a halfhearted attempt, and the end slid off it easily and was climbing Zale's jersey as the scatback heaved the ball toward the speeding Eagle Duvall. The pass was yards short of Duvall, however, and came down in the hands of a surprised but grateful Bruin cornerback. Surprised or not, the Bruin knew which direction to run, and he sprinted all the way into the end zone. The scattered Academy fans slapped one another on the backs. No matter what happened now, the day was a bright one.

"Nice block, Artsy." That was Zale. "You ought to go to a place like Bellevue Academy. Bet you'd fit right in!"

Craig walked off the field fuming. He was angry with Gold, with Zale. But that wasn't it. He was mostly angry with himself, angry and a little ashamed. "You're the quarterback. Act like it!" Duvall had said. That was it.

Muldoon ignored him as he came off, ignored him all the rest of the first half, ignored him, too, in the second half while Al Hanson ran the team up and down the field against the outmanned prepsters. The final score was 48–6, and Muldoon played everyone to keep it that low, even took to punting on third down to give his defensive reserves playing time. It was a beautiful fall day. Craig Warren had never felt worse.

The last week of October. From Craig Warren's bedroom window the rooftops were white with heavy frost as they dropped away street by street down the hill toward the creek. To the west and north the sky deepened in color like a bruise, and the smell of snow was in the wind. When he walked to school the brown leaves sparkled with frost crystals. They crackled underfoot like tissue paper.

Tiny Daugherty was an immense figure, a kind of Russian weightlifter with a cherub's face, a rock-hard belly thrust proudly before him as he shambled down the halls. "Hey, Warren," he burbled cheerily as Craig came in the door. He rushed toward Craig, oblivious to the other students parting before him like a small body of water before an aircraft carrier. Daugherty threw an enormous arm across Craig's shoulders, and the slender

124

quarterback winced. Together they made their way toward class, Craig being knocked off stride every other step by the surge of Daugherty's bulky hip.

Daugherty was in a good mood. "Okay, Warren," he said, beaming with pride. "Quiz time."

"Quiz time?"

"Yeah. Just listen, okay? Bruin quiz time." Daugherty's eyes all but disappeared when he smiled. "Question number one. How can you tell which is the quickest Bruin lineman?"

Craig shook his head. He didn't want to hear about the Bruins, not after Saturday's fiasco.

"Give up?" Daugherty paused. "He's the one who's farthest offside," said Tiny, exploding with laughter and clapping Craig on the back. "Whoo, boy! Get it! The one who's farthest offside!"

Craig laughed as best he could. It didn't pay to frustrate Daugherty's occasional impulses toward a career as a stand-up nightclub comic.

When Tiny's belly stopped shaking, he was ready for another. "Okay," he said, "question number two in your Bruin quiz. Ready? How many Bruin guards pull on their famous end sweep?"

Craig pondered. "Three?"

Daugherty looked suspiciously at his captive audience. "Three? I see. Like there would be only two guards, but Bellevue would have three. That's good. That's all right, Warren. *Wrong*, but all right! Give up?"

Craig sighed and nodded.

Daugherty paused for effect. "Two," he said. "One in each direction!" He frowned. "Do you think it's funnier your way? You know, three, like you said?"

"No," said Craig, "it's better like you have it, Tiny."

Daugherty beamed proudly. "Next question," he an-

125

nounced, ignoring Craig's groan. "How can you tell which Bruin is going to carry the ball?"

"I don't know, Tiny. I—hey, what's going on in front of Mr. Craft's room?"

Daugherty squinted myopically ahead. "Dunno," he said glumly. "Looks like a teachers' meeting." The huge lineman squirmed uneasily. Teachers made him nervous, spoiled his weeks with homework and classes. "I think I'll just tiptoe off that way," he said, accidentally knocking the books from the arms of a passing classmate with a sweep of his paw. Then he was off, making his way up the stairwell marked DOWN while the crowds slowed and swung around him. Halfway up the stairs he stopped, a bulky rock in the stream of passersby. "Hey, Warren," he bellowed. "He's the one with the buzzards circling his helmet!" Then he was gone, his giggle trailing behind him down the stairwell.

The teachers clustered around Mr. Craft were excited and happy, not at all their usual Monday morning selves. The men were pumping his hand and beaming, while the women teachers fluttered around looking pleased with themselves and the world. Mr. Craft himself looked a little dazed at all the attention, but his plump, bearded face was grinning from ear to ear.

As Craig passed the group of teachers, Mrs. Kellogg, his English teacher from sophomore year, gave Mr. Craft a big hug. "I'm so happy for you, Arthur," she said. "You tell Jean I'll be over to see her as soon as things settle down." Then she was off, almost bumping into Craig as she peeled out of the crowd.

"Well, hello there, Craig Warren," she said cheerfully, pushing her glasses up her nose. Craig liked Mrs. Kellogg. She was the oldest teacher in the school, had taught his mother English thirty years before, his father even before that. She wore tweed jackets and sensible shoes. "A handsome woman," Craig's mother always said.

"Did you hear the great news, the splendid news?" asked Mrs. Kellogg. Mrs. Kellogg talked like an English teacher sometimes, but Craig guessed it wasn't any worse than Daugherty's jokes. Just different.

He shook his head.

The crowd of milling students had thinned out now. The bell was about to ring, and he and the English teacher had the hall almost to themselves. "Mrs. Craft, Jean Craft. She just had a baby boy! A perfectly healthy baby boy! The doctors say there's no doubt. No trace of that . . . problem . . . they had last time."

Craig was puzzled. "I guess I don't know about that," he said.

"You don't? No, I guess you wouldn't. None of the students do. Arthur—Mr. Craft—just doesn't bring his troubles to work." She trailed off. The bell rang. Mrs. Kellogg looked at Craig sharply. "Well, some of them *should* know, the things they say about him. I may be old, but I'm not deaf."

She put a hand on Craig's arm, keeping him a moment. "Craig, two years ago Mr. Craft's daughter died. She was only three years old. It almost killed him. He carries this gene, you see—about one out of twenty Americans do. And his wife, too. They didn't know it until the baby . . . well, anyway, the chances are twenty-five percent that any child of theirs would be born with the disease. Do you follow?"

Craig wasn't sure, but he nodded. It made him uneasy, being kept after the bell. Still, things were falling into place. "Bells for John Whiteside's Daughter," and some of the other poems.

"Twenty-five percent," said Mrs. Kellogg fiercely.

"One in four. Can you understand that? The baby was dead and he came to class every day and he never said a word, not to anyone. Went on teaching to kids who didn't know or care about literature—about anything, some of them."

Craig nodded.

"And now they have their baby," said Mrs. Kellogg triumphantly. "Think what courage it took to try again! And he's healthy!" She dabbed at an eye with a crumpled Kleenex. "Oh, Craig, it's right out of the Bible, you know, Deuteronomy: 'I have set before you life and death, blessing and curse; therefore choose life.' "

"Yes, ma'am," said Craig, not knowing what else to say. "I better get to class."

"He's a brave man, your Mr. Craft," Mrs. Kellogg said as Craig started down the hall. "It's a quiet courage, not all that fuss and bonfires, but it's the hardest kind there is."

A quiet courage. The hardest kind there is. A soft, plump man who taught poetry, even cried over it sometimes. Craig Warren had never thought of courage that way.

"Thanks, Mrs. Kellogg," said Craig over his shoulder, not even sure yet for what, as he dashed for class. But already the hallway seemed somehow a little wider.

SIXTEEN

*A*ll set, Bill?" said Muldoon to Coach Buckwalter. "Okay, somebody get the lights."

The Owls were in their locker room, sprawled on benches, and wearing only their practice pants and T-shirts. Muldoon had set the movie screen along one wall and Coach Buckwalter had threaded the projector against the opposite row of lockers.

The Owls were loose. "I hope it's the Roadrunner," whispered Johnny Zale.

"Anyone bring popcorn?" asked Tiny Daugherty.

"Knock it off," bellowed Muldoon. "Now this is a film of Oldfield's game Friday night against Brackenridge. Oldfield's a fine team, a tough outfit." He took his glasses off and eyed Daugherty sourly. "After next Friday, they may be going around school telling Owl jokes, Daugherty. What, you don't think I know what goes on around here? How about 'Who's the softest Owl lineman?' Or 'Biggest creampuff imitating a tackle?'"

Daugherty flushed and was quiet.

The film flashed numbers on the screen, then blurred

players, then a sharper focus. Twenty-two tiny figures on Brackenridge High School's lush field. It was odd to see the game in shades of gray and black, funny to watch the players dance backward when Buckwalter reversed the film. It looked like pass receivers were heaving balls forty yards back over their shoulders to passers who caught them with one hand, ran up to the line, and ducked under the center. The Owls were used to the comic effect, but it was still fun.

"Oldfield's in dark jerseys," said Muldoon. "Brackenridge in white with the dark helmets." Brackenridge had the ball. "Now don't be looking past Oldfield to the Bisons," Muldoon said. "Look sharp at that Oldfield line."

Craig picked out Michelonis. So that was the living legend. Three times All State if he made it this year, and that was sure as the ski slope and winter coming. Craig was surprised. Michelonis wasn't big at all. About Craig's own size in fact, maybe six feet plus and one hundred seventy-five pounds.

Michelonis took the ball and started to his right, and the Oldfield line smothered him. Not as fast as Craig had expected, probably not as fast as Johnny Zale if it came to that. Muldoon's voice came out of the dark. "Now, you see that? That's a good line. Oldfield beats Brackenridge off the ball all night long. And a good game plan for stopping Michelonis, too. Lots of pursuit, good use of keys. Try to make the other players beat you, not 'Iron Mike.'"

It was true, Oldfield was dominating the line of scrimmage. Watching the first quarter wind down, it looked as if *they* were the number one team in the state. They drove steadily down the field, mixing plays nicely. Muldoon stopped the film again and again, had

Buckwalter run back play after play to show how the Oldfield Huskies blocked on a trap or to point to one of the guards who seemed to tip a play by leaning backward when he was assigned to pull out. Then there was an offside, and the Huskies had to punt.

"Watch this," said Muldoon. "I know I said to watch Oldfield, not Brackenridge, but this is something."

The ball sailed down to Michelonis, who caught it at about his own 20 and started running to his right. The other safety crossed behind him and Michelonis seemed to hand him the ball and turn casually to watch his teammate run the reverse to his left. One Oldfield tackler pushed off Michelonis in his haste to pursue the play. The entire Husky team slid frantically toward the new threat. It was as if Michelonis went completely limp, almost as if he became invisible. Then he took off. The Owls in the dark room gasped in surprise. The camera man recovered and followed the small figure in the white jersey with the dark 44 on the back as he dashed down the sideline. Near the goal line, he was overtaken by a speeding defender, but Michelonis rolled off the Oldfield man's tackle as if there were no interference with his momentum at all, went into the end zone standing up. The Owls whistled softly, and somebody broke into quiet applause.

"A touch of genius," said Muldoon. "No other word for it. Only player I've ever seen disappear and then reappear someplace else!" He wiped his glasses. "Now watch this!"

Brackenridge lined up for the extra point. Michelonis jammed his helmet down, rubbed his hands on his pants, gestures, Craig noted, that seemed habitual. The ball was snapped and put down and Michelonis drove it through, then bent down and did something with his shoe.

"Unties it and ties it every time," said Muldoon. "A way of keeping his head down. Every time. You have to feel a little sorry for Holloway, the Oldfield coach. Spends all week saying, 'Stop Michelonis. Never mind those other backs. Give 'em a little. But stop Michelonis.' And what happens? Michelonis stops dead in his tracks, darn near sits down with the paper, and the Oldfield kids about push him out of the way to get to a rinky-dink running back who doesn't even have the ball!" Muldoon chuckled in the dark. "No wonder coaches get old so young!"

As they watched the screen, it was obvious that something went out of the Oldfield Huskies after that. Even on the grainy film, you could sense that they were beaten. They still moved the ball smartly, still slammed into Michelonis with everything they could muster, but the game belonged to Brackenridge. And to Michelonis. Muldoon had Buckwalter back up the play as the Brackenridge tailback ran hard to his right and then, completely without warning, threw a beautiful spiral to a receiver racing in the other direction downfield. "They'll tell you he doesn't have a major college arm," said Muldoon as the receiver danced into the end zone, "but I don't know what else to call *that!*"

Oldfield tried everything. Again and again they pounded the slender tailback, driving him into the turf, hitting him along the sidelines, knocking him into the Bison reserves on the bench. "I hate that," said Muldoon. "I won't have it! No late hits! None of that twisting and gouging! That's garbage, and there won't be any of that at Oiltown while I'm coaching." The glasses were off, and Muldoon tugged at his wiry hair. "When we get to Brackenridge, we'll hit Michelonis with good clean gang tackling. We'll stop him cold. But clean! Or if we can't stop him clean, we'll lose. But we can keep our heads up after it."

The film was running down. Craig Warren couldn't take his eyes off Michelonis, off the small figure in the gray film, who seemed to play with such intensity and joy that he alone blossomed into color. What would it be like, he wondered, to play the game, or any game, like that? Would it be something like what Duvall had said to him outside Thornbush's office building? "I don't want *anybody* to go away feelin' he didn't get every last thing he paid for." Or was it even simpler than that? A superstar father maybe who coached you from the time you could walk? Yes, and throw in a mother who might have been a world-class gymnast or something. Or maybe for Michelonis it was more complex—some union of spirit and body that he could call on in the same way that even quite frail women could occasionally lift an automobile like a human jack to save a child's life. Or maybe deeper still—to places Craig had read about, places usually inhabited only by Zen sword masters and other ancient martial artists: men so at one with life and the ways of its motion that for them it was all dance or play. Yet no attack from any direction could ever surprise them.

At the end, Michelonis had thrown for a touchdown and run for two, and Brackenridge had beaten a strong Oldfield team 28–7. What did Michelonis dream about at night? Craig wondered. Did he hang his uniform in his closet like Superman's cape, yawn, "Ho hum, another terrific game"? What white-eyed monsters did he fake right out of his dreams?

"That's it," said Muldoon. "Saddle up and hit the

133

practice field. Scout team get with Coach Buckwalter. Get ready to be Huskies!"

An hour and a half later, in the coaches' tiny dressing room, Muldoon was running a brush through his tufts of woolish hair. In a corner Buckwalter was humming to himself, knotting his tie.

"Good practice, Bill," said Muldoon. "Scout team did a good job. Gave us the authentic Oldfield look."

"Well," said Buckwalter, "we should have the Huskies down pretty good by now. Holloway's been there, what? Twelve years now? And every year the same thing. Solid, basic football."

Muldoon nodded. "And of course there's no superstar this week. Tougher to get ready next week. No matter who you throw in at tailback on that scout outfit, it's nothing like the real thing, nothing like that Michelonis."

"Dress up your nastiest house cat and call him 'Tiger,'" said Dykstra. "Who'll you use to stand in for Iron Mike? Al Hanson?"

"Cross that bridge when we come to it," said Muldoon. "Would you listen to us? All day long we're yelling at the kids to forget Brackenridge. Telling 'em not to look past Oldfield or they'll get their fannies kicked this Friday night. And here we are, worrying about Michelonis. He won't mean much if we don't get by Oldfield."

"It's a problem," sighed Buckwalter, slipping into his old sport coat, trying to see himself in the mirror around Muldoon's head. "We've had it too easy since McKean. Our kids are looking past Oldfield to the number one team in the state, and there's no convincing them that these Huskies aren't creampuffs."

"Creampuffs, huh?" said Muldoon. "Well, I've got a trick or two up the old sweatshirt sleeve."

134

"Gonna motivate 'em, huh, Coach?" asked Dykstra, with a wink at Buckwalter.

"Motivate, schmotivate," said Muldoon. "I'm just going to make them very, very hostile."

Game day. Winter rain slanted in from the north, from the west. It battered the bare tree branches and turned the leaves to mush underfoot. It rattled windows in the old frame houses in Oiltown, and drenched the yellowed grasses of the ski slope. Rain formed small lakes in the parking lot of Oiltown High School and blew in great gusty sheets across the practice fields and across Owl Stadium, too.

All day Craig Warren watched the rain glumly from the windows of one classroom after another. Even Tiny Daugherty was subdued on a day like this. It was raining and it was going to rain. The hours dragged past, Spanish after geometry. Earth science. Lunch. A study hall. Health. Geography. And finally Mr. Craft's English class. And all the time the sky was an angry charcoal color, and the rain beat steadily against the windowpanes.

Mr. Craft was talking about imagination again, how it grew literal, how it transformed reality, how that was the poet's true work. The class was drowsy. Johnny Zale across the aisle doodled football plays in a notebook. Craig was listening, but he didn't know about that imagination stuff. Let's see Craft imagine the rain away. Still, he wondered about that Saul Bellow thing on the board. He leafed back through his notes. Yes, there it was: "Imagination, imagination, imagination! It converts to actual! It sustains, it alters, it redeems . . . ! What Homo sapiens imagines, he may slowly convert himself to." He wanted to know about that. As low as he was, to be altered or converted to anything at all could only be a step up. He

135

wanted to ask Mr. Craft, but not here, not now. Never in front of Johnny Zale. Zale was as cold and real as the rain beating at the windows. He didn't have to imagine what Craig Warren was. Zale *knew*.

The final bell rang. Craig shuffled down the hall with the rest, put on his coat, took the books he needed for the weekend, and started for the front door. As he passed Mr. Craft's room, he noticed the door was open. Mr. Craft was sitting alone at his desk, leafing through a stack of essays. Craig glanced up and down the hall. Nobody was paying any attention to him. Not an Owl in sight. He stepped quickly into the alcove and knocked on the half-open door.

Mr. Craft looked up and smiled. "Hi, Craig. Come on in. What's up?"

Craig was uneasy. He pulled the door closed behind him. Mr. Craft eyed him quizzically. "Well," Mr. Craft said, "I know it's not trouble with your grade in English. Just looked over your essay. It shows some real thinking. More than thinking, some sensitivity." He sighed. "I wish sometimes you'd share more of that with the class, but—I guess it's hard for you. I understand that."

Craig felt his face grow warm. Mr. Craft knew more than he let on. To change the subject Craig said, "I heard about your new baby. I'm glad. I mean congratulations."

Mr. Craft beamed. "Arthur Junior. Wonderful child! We'll have him reading the *Iliad* by next week. Give him something to do these long nights when he's up and howling at two A.M."

A gust of wind battered the windows. The rain was coming down harder than ever. "Beastly day," said Mr. Craft. "I don't envy you boys having to slosh around out there tonight."

"No," said Craig. "I should get home. Eat. We have to be back for taping and that by six-thirty."

Mr. Craft didn't say anything. Craig took a step toward the door. With his hand on the knob, he paused. "You know those things you put on the board sometimes? From books we don't read or famous authors?"

Mr. Craft nodded. "I didn't think anyone noticed. What about them?"

"Well, this one—" Craig thumbed through his notebook, came out with the quotation about imagination, read it aloud.

Mr. Craft chuckled. "Oh yes. That's a favorite of mine. *Henderson the Rain King*. Great book. Great character, totally larger than life! Reminds me a little of your friend Tiny Daugherty, more of Eagle Duvall."

"Henderson. The Rain King?"

"That's right. Great comic figure. He's a Connecticut millionaire, middle-aged, who ends up rain king in an African village."

"And he says that about imagination?"

Mr. Craft shook his head. "No. His wise friend says that. The real king of the tribe. He has a theory. Let's see—how does he put it? 'It is all a matter of having a desirable model in the cortex'—the brain, you know. Something like that." Mr. Craft paused, then plunged ahead. "To make Henderson more *noble*, more worthy to be rain king, his friend exposes him to lion therapy." Mr. Craft chuckled again. "He makes poor Henderson trot around in a lion's den, roar like the lion, *absorb* the lion, eventually *act* the lion."

"What for?"

"So Henderson can transform himself."

Craig studied the floor. "Does it work?"

Mr. Craft smiled. "Oh no you don't, my friend," he

said. "I've been teaching too long to fall for that! You've gotten everything from me you'll get. The rest you can learn from Mr. Bellow. You'll find him in the public library."

SEVENTEEN

*T*he Owl locker room was warm, warm enough to make them sleepy, and it was dry. From far away the Owls could hear the muffled sounds of the crowd gathering despite the steady rain. No band tonight. They would be there, of course, and cheering, but the instruments and uniforms would stay dry in the band room. The Owls lay on their warm-up capes, sprawled over benches and on the floor. Only a few looked up as Muldoon thrust his way through the door from outside, water cascading from his slicker and running off the ridiculous brim of his battered baseball cap. "Nice weather for ducks—and owls," he announced cheerily, drying his glasses with a handkerchief. Craig noticed he was carrying something under his slicker, something he wanted to keep dry. Then Muldoon was gone, disappearing into the coaches' cubicle. Craig lay back. Probably the familiar Muldoon clipboard.

A moment later Muldoon was back. "All right," he said. "Get your pads on. No sense in coming back in here after we get all wet and ready to go. We'll go out in a few minutes, get loose, and then go after 'em!"

The Owls started dressing, helping one another by pulling the tight white game jerseys down over the bulky shoulder pads. Muldoon waited until even Waldo Frampton had struggled into his uniform, waited until the clatter of pads and cleats was still and all the Owls were seated along the long benches of the bleak room. Some of the players yawned involuntarily, trying to keep Muldoon from seeing. It was a good night to sleep, the patter of autumn rain on the roof.

"Gentlemen," said Muldoon. "Ladies," glaring at the yawners. "I just ran into Jud Holloway, the Husky coach, out there in the hall. Holloway said he's sorry he and I've been feuding these past ten years or so, and he and his team want to make it up to us. Then he gave me this box. Now I don't know what's in it, but he asked me to turn it over to the Owls before the game."

The Owls were awake now. They exchanged glances. Jud Holloway was known to be almost as crazy as Muldoon himself. Still, Muldoon was up to something. He set the box carefully on the floor in the center of the semicircle of benches. Then he ripped it open with a kind of magician's flourish. The Owls pressed in to look.

In the box were a dozen creampuffs, each bearing a tiny slip of paper attached to a toothpick, and on each slip was printed the name of an Owl starter. The twelfth creampuff was labeled "Coach Muldoon." On the inside top of the box someone had lettered SWEETS TO THE SWEET with a heavy marking pen.

There was absolute silence for a moment, and then Waldo Frampton reacted. "Aggghhh!" he screamed, and he leaped with both feet squarely on the creampuffs, spurting cream filling on all sides. He jumped violently again and again on the helpless box, an assault that ended only when he skidded on the filling and took a hard pratfall amid the circle of Owls.

Nobody else said a word. "Well," said Muldoon dryly, polishing his glasses, "at least Frampton is ready to play. Now let's get out there and show 'em who the creampuffs are!" And the Owls clacked on out of the warm locker room into the driving night rain.

The lights of the field had sparkling rings around them and the crowd was muffled and silent under their umbrellas. There were puddles three and four inches deep on parts of the field, and the center portion of the gridiron was soft enough that the Owls sank almost to their shoe tops.

Craig liked warm-up. While Gold loosened up his arm, Craig filled in as a receiver in one of the two lines that alternated in running pass routes. That was fun, though the wet and slippery balls were throwing Gold more than he was throwing them. Pass after pass fluttered short or sailed off in a rising line over the receiver's head. Craig turned to Eagle Duvall, standing just in front of him in line, while the players waited for Billy Krieg to retrieve one of Gold's errant passes from a puddle along the sideline in front of the Owl bench. "Why would Holloway do that?" Craig asked. "About the cream-puffs?"

Duvall eyed Craig suspiciously. "He wouldn't," said Eagle.

"You think Muldoon—"

Eagle grinned. "You should've seen him the night we played Brackenridge last year. Said his job was on the line. Said he'd be fired sure if we didn't beat Brackenridge. Showed us a picture of his wife and son and the three girls. I got all steamed up. Didn't want those kids on the street."

"What happened?"

"Michelonis happened. And Muldoon's still here. I don't even think he *has* kids," said Eagle, dropping into his stance and heading out for a pass that nose-dived into the mud ten yards before it reached him.

Craig smiled. That Muldoon!

Gold tried a few more passes, then gave up in disgust. He and Billy Krieg trotted off to look for a dry spot to work on place kicks. Al Hanson stepped in and took over the passing but he had even less success than Gold. After a half-dozen feeble tries, he gave Craig a nod and slipped embarrassedly into the line of pass catchers. Craig took the ball from a reserve center and dropped back. It wasn't too bad, really. He turned the laces a quarter turn farther into his palm, something he'd learned during his long summer sessions with his oldest ball and the bucket of muddy water, and he adjusted his throwing motion a little. But with the size of his hands, his long and strong fingers, he found he could throw the ball pretty well, even get a little steam on it. Willie White ran a deep route down the middle and Craig whipped his arm through and the ball sailed straight and true into White's sure hands.

"Good shot, Warren," said Coach Buckwalter, who had been watching. Rain beat pleasantly on Craig's helmet. Football was fun. They should outlaw the pass rush.

Jud Holloway's Huskies were no creampuffs, that was certain. They were steaming mad after suffering their first loss of the season the week before, and they intended to make the Owls pay. Holloway had a good game plan. The maroon-jerseyed Oldfield team took the opening kickoff and marched steadily down the field despite the heavy weather. They ran away from Eagle Duvall as much as possible, picked on the young Owl linebackers, were able to trap Tiny Daugherty twice before the immense tackle got wise. In eleven plays they moved the ball to the Oiltown 20. From there they swept the left end for seven, slammed away up the middle for two more. On third and less than a yard, Mitchell, the Husky quarterback, dove over a wet pack of Husky linemen for a first and goal at the 9 yard line. The Owls dug in. Oldfield tried to trap Daugherty again, but Tiny got under the trapping guard and piled up the play after a yard's gain. On the next play Mitchell changed cadence cleverly, and Larry Bizarro slid across the neutral zone and made contact with one of the Husky guards. Flags flew, and the referee walked off half the distance to the goal line. Mitchell then gave it to his fullback, who slipped and slithered through a tiny hole all the way to the one. The band and cheerleaders were pleading with the Owls to "Hold that line!" but Mitchell suckered everyone by faking a handoff and tiptoeing around Duvall's end into paydirt. Duvall stood motionless, hands on hips for at least ten seconds. Then he slowly shook his head in disbelief. As Mitchell trotted slowly back to his huddle, he wagged a taunting finger at Eagle.

The Owl fans were completely silenced, managing only a few dampened cheers when the center snap for the extra point skidded past the holder and wound up floating in a puddle almost at the 20 yard line. Daugherty sloshed after the ball and submerged it by landing on it to kill the play. The Owls hadn't yet touched the ball, and they trailed, 6–0.

Craig sat huddled on the bench while the rain soaked steadily through his black windbreaker. You played against Daugherty, Duvall, White, and, yes, even Pulaski and Bizarro, all week, and they seemed invincible. Nobody could make a sucker out of Eagle Duvall, trap Daugherty with such ease, push Pulaski and Bizarro around the field like the old Waldo Frampton. He couldn't believe what he had seen. Well, now things would turn around.

But the Owls couldn't move the ball at all. Like McKean and Allenville, Oldfield stacked along the line of scrimmage and dared Oiltown to throw the football. With the rain and mud as a twelfth man, the Huskies piled on Johnny Zale every time he touched the football. When Gold tried the reverse with Eagle Duvall carrying, the Oldfield line called the play even before he made the handoff, and Eagle found three or four tough tacklers waiting for him. All the Owls could do was punt and hope for a break.

It wasn't that Oldfield never fumbled. Though the officials changed balls on almost every play and kept the ball under a little tent of towel while the teams huddled, as the field became sloppier underfoot, the balls became slick as pigs in a muddy sty. The trouble was that Gold matched Mitchell fumble for fumble, and the Owls seemed to get the worst of the exchanges.

Finally the Huskies punted the ball dead on the Owl 30 yard line. Zale tried to sweep end and was dumped unceremoniously in a puddle by a pack of Oldfield linemen. "Zale carried," intoned the public-address system. "Stopped by the right side of the Oldfield line. A yard loss on the play."

"Hell's bells," snapped Muldoon. "We've got to throw the ball some. Got to get them to give us running room." He sent Waldo Frampton in with a play. Waldo ducked into the huddle, and Gold backed out and sent a questioning glance to the sideline. Muldoon stared grimly back, and Gold went back to the huddle and called the play.

Gold dropped back into the pocket. It seemed as if all eleven Huskies were rushing him, and Eagle Duvall was wide open over the middle. Gold swung his arm through, but the ball slipped out of his hand as his arm started forward and squirted almost straight up in the air. There was a tangle of maroon arms and hands snapping at the ball like a school of hungry fish, and then one of the Husky ends tucked the slippery football under his arm and sloshed through mud and rain the thirty yards to the Owl end zone. Gold picked himself up from the muck and scraped a fistful of mud from the bars of his face mask. Then he slammed the ball of mud furiously to the ground.

"His best throw of the night," said Dykstra to Buckwalter.

"Yeah," said Buckwalter. "At least he hit the ground."

The Husky quarterback tried to roll around Duvall's end for the two-point conversion, and the Eagle drilled him, driving him into a swampy patch along the sideline with such force that the two of them skidded fifteen yards along the wet turf, a huge rooster tail of water rising behind them. The crowd cheered, but it had a damp and hollow sound to it. The Owls went in at halftime wet, miserable, and behind 12–0.

The sodden creampuffs were still oozing filling in the center of the locker room, and a few of the players kicked at the mess as they filed dispiritedly toward the circle of gray benches. Tiny Daugherty sank wearily down and glared balefully at Waldo Frampton. "*Doggone* it, Frampton," he sighed. "Why do you have to be so gung-ho?" He nodded his massive head in the direction of the ruined creampuffs. "Right about now, I'd like to eat mine."

As Craig watched the second half, the rain had eased up at last, but the air was thick with fine mist. It was like breathing water. The game was strange, not like football, but more like a bunch of kids fingerpainting or playing with mudpies. You got muddy and wet, then muddier and wetter, and after a while that seemed to be the whole point of the game.

"Stay close to 'em," Muldoon had said at the half. "Play defense! Hit harder! Reach back and get a little extra! Don't wait for a break! Don't pray for a break! *Make* a break!" He had also made a defensive adjustment, letting Eagle Duvall line up at left end on one play, right end on the next, usually to the wide side of the field, so that Oldfield would have to guess where he was going to be, run away from him to the short side where the sideline waited like an extra linebacker. The tactic was working. Oldfield was bogged down in mud and Owls. Still, time was on Mitchell's side. He was content to punt and keep the clock running. Even at the end of the third quarter nothing had changed. The Huskies still led 12–0 as the teams changed ends of the field. The crowd was in an uproar, pleading with the Owls to "Get something going!"

The Oldfield quarterback had a tough decision. He had the ball, third and less than two, on his own 28 yard line. He wasn't going to throw the ball, not in this slop, not with a two-touchdown lead, and the Owls were tossing back every ballcarrier he thrust at them from tackle to tackle. He stuck his head up out of the huddle. Where was that Duvall? Mitchell took a chance. He called the same bootleg that had worked for a touchdown in the first half. This time, though, he'd run away from Duvall.

The Husky quarterback took the ball and made his fake to a running back, but it was a sloppy fake, the back slipping just as he was supposed to be taking the ball, and the Owls had the play diagnosed. Mitchell tried to get to a sideline, saw he couldn't make it, hesitated a second, teetering as he balanced precariously in the treacherous footing as he started to cut back. He never saw Eagle Duvall coming, and the muscular end had a long run before he arrived with tremendous force to slam into the Oldfield quarterback. The ball popped loose and Willie White outscrambled three or four maroon shirts to flop on top of it for the Owls. Duvall tapped Mitchell on his gold helmet with the maroon stripe and yanked the groggy quarterback to his feet. "Awww, look at that," said Eagle. "You got all muddy. Now what will Mummy say?"

But the Owls were still twenty yards from a touchdown. They got half of it the easy way when the Huskies nailed Johnny Zale along the sideline and one of their linebackers couldn't resist getting in an extra hit on the Owl tailback when he was already well out of bounds. Muldoon glowered. "That's Holloway for you. Same stuff they pulled on Michelonis. Late hits, a lot of dirty stuff. In the end that kind of garbage always costs you plenty!"

On the next play Gold, afraid of a fumble, tried a quarterback sneak and found a small seam between Mark Thomas and Paul Pulaski. The ex-fullback plowed through, kept his feet churning, piled into the safety man at the 5 and went down kicking and lunging just short of the goal line. Muldoon jammed a fist into the damp air. "Take that, Holloway," he snapped. "You'll never beat me!"

Still taking no chances on a fumble, Gold took the ball himself twice more, leaping over the tangled wall of linemen on third down for the Owls' first score of the night. Muldoon looked at the clock. Only about four minutes to go. Gold came to the sideline. "Is it dry enough to kick?" Muldoon asked.

Gold shrugged. "Beats trying to pass," he said.

Pulaski's snap wobbled back and Billy Krieg made a great play to trap the ball and get it on the tee. Gold's foot swung through and the kick knuckle-balled crazily just inside the left upright, scraping the crossbar as it passed.

"I'll take it," said Muldoon.

The Owls were fired up now, the crowd driving them on, and the Huskies were tired. The kickoff squad penned the Oldfield return team deep in Oldfield territory, Waldo Frampton making the tackle, and they came to the sideline with a lot of shoulder slapping and cheering as the defense hurried out onto the muddy field. Gold and Muldoon and Buckwalter conferred on the sideline. "Can you throw the ball at all, Goldie?" Buckwalter asked.

Gold held up a short, muscular hand. "I just can't get a grip, Coach," he said mournfully. "No way. Nobody can throw it tonight."

"Well, we need a big play," said Muldoon. "They've seen the Duvall reverse."

"Warren!" said Buckwalter.

"How's that?" said Muldoon.

"In warm-up. I watched him. Warren was throwing the ball around like it was noon in the Sahara."

There was a cheer from the crowd as the Owl defense stymied the Huskies for a third consecutive time. A little more than two minutes left. The Huskies lined up in punt formation, taking their time, willing to risk a delay of game penalty to run the clock down as far as possible.

The Owls made a furious rush to get at the Oldfield punter, but the kicker got it away quickly and pretended to swoon as the onrushing line swerved to avoid him.

There were no flags. "Good act, son," said the referee as he trotted past the prone Husky toward midfield where the kick had slid out of bounds.

Gold tried the middle for three yards. Zale, fighting for everything he could get, hammered his way for his longest gain of the night, coming up just short of the first down. The chains came out and the official held up one hand with the thumb and first finger about two inches apart. The crowd was on its feet. Muldoon called time.

Gold came to the sideline. "Warren," barked Muldoon. Craig rose, his black cape behind him on the bench. "Buckwalter says you can throw this wet ball a little."

Craig nodded.

"Well, go in there and throw it then. Go in for DeSales. Goldie, you line up as fullback. Run a thirty-six pass, and Gold, you make that fake *good*, you hear me?"

Gold nodded. Muldoon turned to Craig. "And Warren, you'll only have one man out, Billy Krieg, and if he's covered, you throw it out of bounds. Got it? We can still pick up that first down if we miss the pass. But if you get sacked back there. Or throw an intercept—" Muldoon broke off, drawing a finger across his throat. "Got it now? Warren, please say 'Yessir.'"

"Yessir," said Craig. He could barely get it out.

Gold called the play in the huddle. The Owls looked worried. The clock showed a minute, maybe a little less, as they came to the line. The huge maroon line of Oldfield noticed the change in the Owl backfield. Noticing Gold's change in position, the stocky middle linebacker, a cagey veteran with tape on both hands and blood on the bridge of his nose, screamed, "Watch number twelve!" The Owls had lined up with two tight ends and only Billy Krieg flanked to the right. The Owls needed this first down and it figured that Gold was the big back they needed to get it for them. "Rookie quarterback," shouted the Oldfield middle guard. "Watch for a fumble!"

Craig was calling signals. "Down. White thirty-six. White thirty-six. Hut-hut-hut." Then he had the ball and was spinning to fake it to Gold. And the big back did a tremendous job, "Best play of the night," Muldoon would say watching films the next Monday. As Craig thrust the ball at his stomach, Gold folded his arms over and dove onto the piled up tangle of players who were surging toward him in the off-tackle hole. When they flung him back, he kept his feet and lunged forward again, lower this time, head up, feet churning, battling for a phantom first down as if it meant everything. He would have had it, too, if he'd had the ball.

And out on the flank Billy Krieg was being as lazy as Gold was being industrious. Krieg took a few tentative steps toward the Husky cornerback, who eyed him warily for a second, then turned with Krieg to watch Gold battle for the precious inches that might mean the ballgame. Then Krieg shot forward past the startled defender and was gone along the right sideline.

Meanwhile Craig had carried out his fake and was dropping back with the ball on his hip. For once, there was no pass rush. The Oldfield line had committed itself almost entirely to stopping Clint Gold. Craig turned. There was Billy Krieg dashing down the sideline. The ball was muddy and slick, but no worse that the slick model he had wet down with his bucket two or three times a week all summer.

He didn't have time to think. "Pass!" bellowed Jud Holloway from the Oldfield sideline, and his big line reacted quickly, but Craig was already stepping forward, shifting his weight from his right foot to the left, bringing his arm through like a whip, turning his fingers over hard so that the palm of his hand was actually facing out when he completed his follow-through.

The ball sailed through the rainy air and connected with Billy Krieg just five steps shy of the end zone. Craig waited for Krieg to juggle and drop the slippery ball, but the end looked it all the way into his hands and tucked it away. Craig glanced around for a yellow flag. There was none. He waited to wake up, to find out he was dreaming. And then the Owls landed on him, pummeling him, driving him into the sloppy mud, rubbing his jersey with grimy hands, making him one of them for a moment. He fought his way up, taking his time. There were rainbows around every floodlight towering in the night sky. "Pass complete," said the tinny voice in the sky, "from number nineteen, Craig Warren, to number eighty-three, Billy Krieg. Touchdown on the play." And then everything was rainbows, even the torn, muddy grass of Owl Stadium.

Pandemonium! The locker room was steaming, and the Owls were at their raucous best. Finally Muldoon fought his way through the crowd of jubilant footballers and climbed onto one of the gray benches. The cheering rose, and the chant began. "We're number one! We're number one!" Muldoon gestured for silence, finally getting something only a little louder than the rumble in a busy cafeteria at lunchtime.

"Men," he shouted, "that was a great game! Great game!" He grinned wickedly. "Jud Holloway just told me that was the greatest comeback he'd ever seen! 'Don't have a drop of blood left in me,' he said." The Owls howled with delight.

"Next week it's Brackenridge and Mr. Michelonis.

Then we'll see who's number one! But tonight you really showed me something. Just a great performance under miserable conditions!"

"Must have been those creampuffs, Coach," said Eagle Duvall, looking serious.

"Lord, yes," said Willie White. "They sure got *me* fired up!"

And the rest of the jubilant, happy Owls cracked up. After a minute or two, even Muldoon joined in.

EIGHTEEN

Saturday *morning. Cold and distant sunlight on the* bare tree branches. There were puddles everywhere, dimpled by wind, but the sky was a bleak and empty blue.

Craig Warren's father was sitting in the old kitchen, reading the *Journal.* He smiled broadly as Craig shuffled sleepily in from the dining room. The table was set for breakfast, and Mrs. Warren was busily stirring eggs at the stove.

" 'Bout time you got up, bub," said Craig's father. "Thought you were gonna sleep the weekend away."

"That's a brisk wind," said his mother.

"Hey, bub, sit down here. Have a look at this paper. Feast the old eyes on Carl Carmen's column."

Craig pulled out a chair, rubbed his eyes to clear them of sleep, and glanced at the paper his father thrust under his nose. There was the headline: OWLS EDGE HUSKIES, 13–12. And there was a picture of Clint Gold diving over a heap of "unidentified tacklers" for the Owls' first score. Carl Carmen's column was in the lower corner. LAST

GASP WAS ENOUGH FOR OWLS, the headline said. Then the column began.

> The Owls call him "Artsy-Craftsy," a tribute to his artful passes and crafty fakes. The program lists him as Craig Warren, junior quarterback and non-letterman. But the rangy reserve was the man of the hour last night, coming off the bench with a cannon hidden in his right sleeve and larceny in his heart, as he stole the ballgame out from under the noses of a pack of Oldfield Huskies who had been sniffing victory from the opening kickoff . . .

Craig groaned. Where did Carl Carmen get that Artsy-Craftsy stuff? Now he'd hear about that again all week. "A tribute to his artful passes and crafty fakes." About as accurate as anything else Carl Carmen wrote, Craig guessed.

"How do you like *that*, bub?" beamed his father, slapping the table with his hand. "The old cannon-up-the-sleeve trick, eh?"

His mother bustled from the stove to the kitchen table with a plateful of eggs and bacon. "I suppose a tired metaphor is better than none," she said. "Mr. Carmen writes abominably. But then," she went on, "I shouldn't imagine that it takes him more than six minutes to do one of his columns." She shook her head. "Done properly, writing is the hardest work in the world." Then she smiled quickly and sat down to eat. "You never told us you had a nickname, Craig," she said.

The conversation in the Warrens' warm kitchen was not the only rehash of the Oldfield game that morning. Joe

Hugo and his merry band were out again, defying the wintry wind that swept down Main Street. Not everyone was especially merry.

"They was lucky," said Quick Keller.

"Better than bein' good sometimes," said Dude Perenchio.

"How about this kid, this Warren?" asked Funny Phelps. "He good, or is he lucky?"

"Considerin' it was the first pass he's completed all year, I'd say lucky," said Keller sourly.

"He can throw the ball," said Joe Hugo. "Trouble is, Muldoon told me once, that's *all* he can do."

"How'd Brackenridge make out last night?" someone wanted to know.

"Won. Beat Fort Steel twenty-four to nothing, I think it was."

Cars droned past along Route 219. The sun glinted dully in the dirty shop windows.

"Michelonis? How'd he come out?"

Keller laughed. "Oh, he had himself a bad night. Two touchdowns is all. And a field goal."

"How's he do it?" asked Phelps.

"I think he uses mirrors is how," said Keller. "He ain't that fast, just can't nobody tackle him."

"It's up here," said Joe Hugo, tapping his balding head. He stared off at the hills thoughtfully. "I dunno," he said. "I used to work with a fella name of Burgoyne, 'Gentleman John,' they called him, on a oil lease down south of here. Near McKean it was."

"Wasn't there a Burgoyne played for Brackenridge a while back?" asked Perenchio.

"The same. That was his kid. Played fullback for Brackenridge three years ago, big strapping kid. Used to come down, help out at the rig some weekends." Hugo hitched his belt over his expanse of stomach. "Anyhow, the old man was telling me once how Brackenridge had the ball on the one yard line in a game with McKean. And they give it to his kid. Nothin'! So they give it to him again. Nothin'! Now mind you, this is a big kid, a senior. Michelonis is a freshman. And Michelonis turns to this Burgoyne, this power back, and he says to him, 'The trouble with you, Jack, is you think those defensive linemen are there! They *ain't* there!'"

Quick Keller snorted. "Sounds like one of them yogis," he said.

Joe Hugo shrugged. "So, Burgoyne tells me, his kid says, 'Well, hotshot, let's see you do better, then!'"

"And?"

"And Michelonis goes in standing up. Standing up! Didn't anyone *touch* him! Maybe it *is* mirrors. Maybe he's some kind of yogi, all right. Whatever he is, there ain't but one of him. Call roll and there's only his one name. Michelonis."

Muldoon scowled into his coffee cup. "I can't see it," he said. Behind him in the coaches' dressing room the chalkboard was a hodgepodge of X's and O's with players' names half-erased and other names hastily scrawled atop the erasures.

"He's got the size," said Gene Dykstra, pulling on one of the heavy gray sweatsuits with PROPERTY OHS FOOTBALL stamped on the back.

"And who else can throw it?" added Bill Buckwalter. "Plus," he went on, "you hold a clock on him, the two of them will run the forty in almost the same."

Muldoon sighed. With a practiced flick of the wrist, he propelled his crumpled coffee cup across the small room and into the wastebasket by the equipment room door. "Yeah, but Michelonis, he's the original kamikaze kid. And this one here—" he gestured vaguely at the door, "who knows what he is?"

"Well, who else then?" asked Buckwalter.

"Who else?" asked Dykstra.

Muldoon pushed back from the table and stood up. "I suppose that's what assistants are for," he said. "Have somebody to blame when something doesn't work." He picked up a large box from the table. "Let's get out there. Can't get ready for Brackenridge sitting around in here where it's warm."

The coaches clacked across the cement floor of the equipment room and on into the Owls' locker room. The team was dressed in full pads, ready to head on out to the practice field. They pulled benches around to face Muldoon and his assistant coaches.

"Okay," said Muldoon. "I don't have to make a speech to get you up for this one. Brackenridge is the number one team in this state. Some idiot bunch of sportswriters thought it would be funny to pick you ladies as number two. I *assume* you can all manage a certain level of interest in Friday night's game. Now, when we go out there, we're going to make a few changes in honor of Mr. Michelonis." He pulled another chalkboard from a corner and scribbled quickly while the chalk squeaked and skipped.

"Here," he said. "We're getting tired of watching teams run away from you, Eagle. So we're going to put you here," the chalk jabbed at the middle linebacker spot, "where they *can't* run away, and they can't hide." Muldoon sketched the charges and angles of the down linemen. "See, we're going to protect Eagle with the front five, make a funnel for Michelonis to run into. When he hits the line, Duvall is going to be there like his face in the mirror every morning." Muldoon brought his right fist into his left palm with a sharp pop.

"And don't expect Duvall to do it all," Dykstra broke in. "Every man on the field keeps after Michelonis until you hear a whistle. When you think he's stopped, that's when he's just starting to get dangerous! And don't be afraid to hit him *high*. He's got awfully quick feet out there, and he can make you look real bad if you start reaching or diving."

"Gang tackles," said Muldoon. "Clean. Legal. But everybody after a piece of him *every* play. Because, boys, I'll tell you this. He's looking for a touchdown on *every* play! This is the most determined back you'll ever play against."

"A real challenge," said Buckwalter.

"We're going to go out there now," said Muldoon. "Scout team get blue scrimmage jerseys out of the box, get together with Coach Buckwalter. Give us a good picture of Brackenridge."

The players stood up, began to move toward the door. "One more thing!" shouted Muldoon. The players turned back impatiently. "Warren," said Muldoon, "give the devil his due, you won one for us last Friday. And God love you, 'cause we're throwing you to the lions this week."

He fished around in the box at his feet. "Where is it?" he grumbled. "Ah!" He pulled out a blue game jersey with a bright orange double 4 on the front and back. It was a perfect replica of the Brackenridge uniform except that where the Brackenridge team had BISON in orange just above the front numerals, this jersey had MIKE in the same shade. "Same company makes theirs that makes ours," explained Muldoon with a grin. "I got 'em to throw this in with our new order." He tossed the jersey to Craig Warren. "Here you go," he said. "It's maybe a little big, but this week you're 'Iron Mike.'"

Johnny Zale snorted loudly.

Muldoon whirled toward his running back. "I didn't hear you laughing much last Friday night, Zale," he said icily. "You ran like a marshmallow salesman with his pants slipping. Oldfield is still wondering why Johnny Zale never showed up for last week's game. Now let's get out there!"

The players rumbled out. Muldoon fished around in the box another second and came out with a helmet painted Brackenridge blue. "This should fit," he said. He tossed it to Craig. Someone had carefully spray-painted a silhouette of an orange buffalo on the helmet sides.

"You can thank your pal, Coach Buckwalter, for this," said Muldoon, with a nod at his assistant. "He seems to think you can dress up like Michelonis and give us a decent imitation. See if you can make Bill look like a genius." And the coaches trooped out. "Hustle it up," Dykstra said over his shoulder as the door slammed.

Craig looked down at the jersey in his hands. He knew about being "Iron Mike" for the scout team the week of the Brackenridge game. Last year three different players had had the job, and all three had wound up bruised and limping. What was it Muldoon had said? "We're throwing you to the lions."

Slowly he peeled off his heavy practice jersey. He pulled on the blue game shirt. He was scared, but it felt good anyway. He ran his long fingers over the orange numbers, the lettering. "Mike, huh?" He jammed on the blue-and-orange helmet. It was strange to look down and see this, this—costume. He felt like an actor, not a football player. He raised his eyes to the mirror on the

159

wall by the door. Muldoon had bolted it to the wall together with a sign that read WILL YOU BE ABLE TO LOOK HIM IN THE EYE *AFTER* THE GAME? Craig didn't know the apparition in the mirror. He seemed larger, easier in his movements, more sure of himself. Forty-four. MIKE. Dress rehearsal. He jammed down the helmet, slammed his thigh pads with his large hands. The figure in the mirror gave him a quick, almost imperceptible wink.

Iron Mike! Imagine *that!*

Then Craig Warren opened the door and headed for the lions' den.

NINETEEN

The blue-clad scout team was huddled around Coach Buckwalter at the 20 yard line. "First and ten," Muldoon sang out. "All right, Brackenridge, let's see you move that ball down the field."

And along the line of scrimmage, the Owl varsity defense was ready. More than ready. Craig had never seen them more fired up, Duvall and Daugherty, all of them. Willie White was moving into Duvall's end spot, excited about the chance to get more playing time. They were all pounding one another on the pads and pawing at the stony turf of the practice field. Behind the far end zone the mustard-colored grass of the ski slope waved in the steady November wind like a section of pom-pom girls. Craig's stomach was tingling as if electricity were running through him. He wiped his hands on his jersey front, found them still damp.

Buckwalter was explaining the play, showing the scout team how Brackenridge lined up like a wing-T outfit, the quarterback under center, but that the center made a direct snap to Michelonis or the big fullback most of the time. "It's the old single-wing," Buckwalter was saying, "only with a balanced line, and the quarterback can and will take the center snap and run options and other T-formation plays. But the rest is single-wing. Power sweep, off-tackle, reverse to the wingback, even the old bucklateral where the fullback takes the direct snap, hits the line while slipping the ball to the quarterback, and the quarterback pitches it to Michelonis. Got it?"

The scouts nodded. They eyed the defense apprehensively. It was awfully *noisy* on that side of the line today.

They broke the huddle. Buckwalter had outlined a basic off-tackle slant to the right. Craig could feel his heart thumping a few hundred times a minute as Al Hanson called the signals. Then the ball floated back, high and to his left, and he had it and was moving toward the space just inside his own end where there was supposed to be a hole. He felt himself flinching, hesitating momentarily, and he was stumbling as he met a hurtling Eagle Duvall just behind the line of scrimmage. Duvall had him in the air and two other Owls lunged in for the kill as Craig crashed backward to the stony ground. All the breath left his body, and for a second he thought, "This is what it's like to be dead."

When he opened his eyes, Coach Buckwalter was bending over him. Everything was very bright, as if someone had turned on banks of floodlights behind the grayish purple of the autumn clouds. "You okay, 'Iron Mike'?" Buckwalter was grinning. "C'mon, Mike, we gotta have *you!*" That was Waldo Frampton.

"All set?" yelled Muldoon. "I make it second and twelve, Brackenridge."

There was a buzzing in his ears, something like a bell, almost like speech. He felt that the blue helmet was talking to him. And the jersey, even just the jersey.

Wasn't it breathing to its own rhythm, slower, calmer? Buckwalter was outlining another play. Craig jammed his helmet down, wiped his hands on his thigh pads. Imagination playing tricks? Maybe. But the jersey seemed to go on breathing to its own powerful count, and the helmet. What was it saying? Something about how they'd all come out to see him, were counting on him. The yell leaders. The band. The kids and their fathers, all of them sitting up there behind the cloudy floodlights in the cold and dark, yelling *MIKE MIKE MIKE* not knowing what it costs, while you HIT and SPIN and keep your feet and HIT once more.

"First down," said someone a long way off. "Let's get after it, defense!"

Because it wasn't just himself. It's all of it. And not just Brackenridge. All the other schools, chanting *WIN WIN WIN*, meaning stop *MIKE MIKE MIKE*, stop the Iron Man, HIT him and HIT him and HIT him until . . .

"Second and one." The same distant voice. "Come on, ladies!"

Ringing. Like talking bells. And their bands and cheerleaders and pep rallies, all the special defenses. Duvall one week, the big Polish kid from Coal Creek, those quick little linebackers from McKean. For all of them. Not just for yourself, but for them. You owe it. They need you to be MIKE, to RUN hard and HIT and keep running and NOT go down.

Whistles. "*Another* first down! Hell's bells, what's the matter? Warren too much for you?"

Jam that helmet down. Make sure the hands are dry. No fumbles now. And, in another way, isn't it *all* for you? The music, the cheers, the newspapers? Not that it matters, not those things. What matters is what it makes you do. How it lifts you up, all of them coming at you, all that energy and intensity. Nothing like it, really. What they give you, what you give them, so you can RUN and HIT or stop and—LOOK—a blue shirt wide open downfield and WHIP the arm through. Because it's all for you.

"First and goal! You're not listening, Zale! We've told you and told you about that option pass. Better wake up!"

You owe it to them. Because you're the man. Nobody else can. And this is your time. This is your season. They need you to talk about. To dream of being. To remember years after. HIT and RUN HARD. And all that talk about WIN WIN WIN, what is it but an excuse for the bright grass and lights and the magic DANCE you do when they all come out to STOP MIKE but what they want, really want, is to see him RUN!

Muldoon slammed his clipboard to the turf. "That's the worst I've ever had my number one defense play on a Monday afternoon!" he thundered. "These scouts are walking through you like a gopher through a cow patty!"

Buckwalter took Craig by the arm and bent his craggy face close to the reserve quarterback. He peered in through the bars of the face mask. "That you in there, Warren?" he asked with a smile.

Craig Warren wasn't sure. But behind his mask, *somebody* slipped the coach a huge, smiling wink.

All that long practice week he put on the blue jersey. He played Michelonis three wintry days while the afternoons shrank in the cold and the sky turned lead-colored and heavy. Only when it was too dark to see, only when passes were bouncing off receivers unable to penetrate the gloom, did Muldoon's whistle cut through the raw wind to send them all thankfully to the hot showers.

Each night he walked home alone. The trees were bare

now, and the stars seemed to be moving very fast in the spaces among the dark, violent clouds. New cuts stung in the cold air. He was more aware of his body, how it moved, what each muscle did, than he had ever been in his life. Even his bruises had bruises. He had never felt better.

The halls were full of Michelonis. Banners were everywhere. Stuffed dummies with 44's of tape or paint front and back. Huge Owls munching on tiny Bison. And the paper was full of him. Carl Carmen had a column, some crazy story about Michelonis saying "They ain't there" about somebody or other's line and then proving it by waltzing through it for a touchdown. Michelonis shooting for seven thousand career yards. Michelonis the three-time All-Stater. And pictures of Michelonis. Craig got in trouble with his mother by cutting them out. One of them had part of her crossword puzzle on the back, but in the end she just sighed. "Football!"

Craig taped one of the pictures to his mirror, another to the wall by his bed. Michelonis was the last thing he saw at night, the first thing he saw when he woke up.

Then back to practice and the blue jersey. He began to *absorb* Michelonis, take the orange number and make it a part of himself. He wanted the week never to end. And Muldoon was full of Michelonis. When Michelonis was on defense, Muldoon wanted his offside tackles and ends going downfield to block him on every play. "Make him do some tackling," Muldoon said to his backs. "Throw it long some," he said to Gold. "Make Michelonis run *without* the ball every chance we get." Wear the legend down, that was the idea. Keep him playing defense. And when he did get the ball, Eagle Duvall would be waiting. Everyone would be.

Last-period class. Mr. Craft was still on poetry, today a poem by Robert Frost, not "Stopping by Woods" or the one about two roads in a yellow woods, the ones in the textbook, but a different one, one he'd made copies of and handed out. Most of the class was bored, ready to go home. They stared out the windows at the yellowed grass, the bare branches of the maples on the lawn. Johnny Zale seemed to be dozing in the back of the room. Craig kind of liked the poem. In it someone promised to take you back "out of all this now too much for us" to a farm and a house that weren't a farm and a house anymore. Whoever it was said he "only had at heart your getting lost," and as you followed his voice through the poem, you went along a worn-out road, through a woods, and past a ghost town. When you came to the place, not much was there. Just a cellar hole with a lilac tree, some broken toy dishes under a pine some children once used as a playhouse. Even the field around the farmhouse had shrunk to nothing much. Mr. Craft was finishing the poem, reading it out loud, his plump hands dancing as he spoke.

Your destination and your destiny's
A brook that was the water of the house,
Cold as a spring as yet so near its source,
Too lofty and original to rage.
(We know the valley streams that when aroused
Will leave their tatters hung on barb and thorn.)
I have kept hidden in the instep arch
Of an old cedar at the waterside
A broken drinking goblet like the Grail
Under a spell so the wrong ones can't find it,
So can't get saved, as Saint Mark says they mustn't.
(I stole the goblet from the children's playhouse.)

Here are your waters and your watering place.
Drink and be whole again beyond confusion.

Craig liked to hear Mr. Craft read, even though Zale and the rest liked to make fun of him. He didn't read it like an actor or anything, trying to make his voice something it wasn't. You heard things in the poem when he read, a kind of music that told you what it meant, even if you didn't understand every sentence.

Waldo Frampton had his hand up. Good old Waldo. Even on a long Thursday afternoon you could count on him to be in there trying, English class or football scrimmage. "Now that's more like it," Waldo said. "This poem here's the first one we've read this whole fall where the poet doesn't sound like he's gonna die of being sorry for himself. I like that ending. It's as good as church, almost."

Mr. Craft nodded. "You mean the hints of communion?"

It was Waldo's turn to nod. "Yeah. Getting saved and like that. Being whole again. That's a happy thing to end with."

Dale Davis was frowning. She put her hand up uncertainly.

"Dale?"

"I'm not so sure. I don't trust this guy—this narrator. All he does is take us back to a wreck of a house, a hole in the ground, really. And then he doesn't give you any *Grail*, just something broken he stole from an old playhouse. It's phony. And if it's broken, maybe you *can't* drink out of it anyway."

"You're not sure you'd buy a used Grail from this man, eh?" said Mr. Craft. Johnny Zale woke enough to groan

167

loudly from the back of the room. As usual, Mr. Craft ignored him and went on. "Well, perhaps you shouldn't. After all, what kind of a guide wants to get you lost?"

Craig was interested now. There was something floating around in his mind that he couldn't quite make hold still. Frost and the Grail and the children's house of make-believe and even Mike Michelonis.

"Craig?"

He hadn't raised his hand, but he was caught. Mr. Craft was looking at him expectantly.

"Maybe Waldo and Dale are both right," Craig said slowly. Zale snickered. "It's *like* the Grail, isn't it? And he got it from the pretend house. Maybe if you pretend it's the Grail, you know, make-believe it, it works. And if you can't, or you don't, it doesn't."

"Ah," said Mr. Craft. "So if you can't make it by belief, as the children made their world by belief, are you perhaps one of 'the wrong ones' who can't get saved?"

Craig didn't know. He felt the back of his neck reddening. He made sure his hands were wedged crossways under his biceps. "Maybe the wrong ones are the ones who can't imagine a play goblet is a real Grail," he said.

"I like that," said Mr. Craft as the bell rang. The class began gathering books, shuffling paper. Above the general hubbub, Mr. Craft asked, "Have you managed to get to the library, Craig? I thought perhaps the book I mentioned by Bellow might have given you some ideas about Frost's poem."

Craig shook his head. Out of the corner of his eye he glimpsed Johnny Zale's sneering face. Now he'd done it. When would he learn to keep his mouth shut? Mr. Craft had cooked him again.

TWENTY

Thursday practice was always light. The players pulled on their heavy gray sweatsuits against the cold, put on their black helmets, and went out to the soft turf of Owl Stadium. Craig put on the blue-and-orange game jersey for the last time. On Thursdays the Owls worked on the kicking game, put the special teams through their paces, worked on timing. The little things that won and lost football games. Today, even with no contact planned, Michelonis was the focus of attention. Again and again Muldoon, Dykstra and Buckwalter stressed the importance of kicking the ball away from number 44, of getting downfield fast, but without overrunning the ball. That meant not to end up getting down so fast that you took yourself out of the play without even being blocked. They talked about angles of pursuit, and the importance of helping one another when tackling Michelonis. "They're going to be giving him the ball all night long," said Muldoon, "and we can't keep it away from him when they're on offense. But we can sure try not to give it to him ourselves on our punts and kickoffs!"

Craig enjoyed running back punts. By now it was a ritual, the donning of the blue jersey, the jamming down of the helmet, wiping the hands on the thighs. He tried to do the things he had seen Michelonis do on film, the changes of speed and direction, the fakes that involved going "dead" for an instant and then putting himself in high gear.

The punt angled away from him, but he raced across the field and took it on a short bounce just before it went out of bounds. He turned, as he had seen the All-State tailback do in the Oldfield film, and surveyed the onrushing defenders quickly as they closed in. Craig took one step as if to shoot along the sideline, then cut sharply to his left, giving a little ground to get running room. Not many backs would dare to do that, but for Michelonis it was everyday stuff. Eagle Duvall was the first Owl down, but Craig had learned something during the week that surprised him. He was faster than Eagle. Not much, that was sure, but just enough to get him outside Duvall's turning radius and enable him to turn back upfield with some running room. He slid past Daugherty, trying to keep his feet under him and keep them moving quickly, almost dancing, the way Michelonis did it. He slowed momentarily, let Johnny Zale get a bead on him, then shot forward again, leaving Zale behind. When two or three of the Owls cornered him against the sideline, he tried to cut back, ignored their dummy scrimmage bumps and shoves, and headed for the end zone.

Muldoon's whistle trilled. "That's a good effort, Warren. Too many of you ladies quit on the play," he glowered. "Zale, when you miss, keep after it. I've seen the same tackler miss 'Iron Mike' twice on the same play and get him on the third try. Get to your feet, keep after him, assume he's still running till you hear a whistle!"

As Zale passed Craig Warren, he lowered his voice. "Way to go, Artsy. You're a real dummy scrimmage hero!"

It was like waking up from a dream of summer vacation to a cold Monday morning in February. Zale had a way of making you smaller, reminding you who people thought you were, bringing you back to reality.

Most of the fun went out of practice for Craig then, and he was glad when Muldoon called a halt with a half-hour's daylight left. Muldoon called them all into a circle. He eyed the Owls for a long minute. Then he said, "Boys, the hay's in the barn. We've done all we can do to get you ready. No creampuffs this Friday night. No bonfire. No pep rally. It's up to you. If you want to be the number one team in this state, you'll have to play the game of your lives. It's there for the taking." And he sent them in.

When the Owls came straggling out of the locker room on their ways home, the light had turned a deep shade of lavender. The air was ringing with snow that wouldn't fall, but you knew it was there.

"Paper says snow tomorrow night," Tiny Daugherty said.

"I didn't know you could read, Daugherty," said Johnny Zale. Daugherty good-naturedly swung a heavy hip into Zale, a Saint Bernard brushing off a puppy, and the running back crashed into Craig Warren.

Zale turned, pulling on the ends of a towel he had draped around his neck. "Well, well," he grinned. "Artsy-Craftsy. Hey, Artsy, you were *very* good in class today." He mimicked Mr. Craft fiercely. "I say, Warren old pip, have you been to the library for those books I've set aside?"

Craig didn't say anything. Zale slapped him on the back, hard. "That's all right, Warren. You just keep sucking up to those English teachers. They're just your style."

"Craft must be okay," somebody said. "He just had a baby and all."

"Yeah?" snickered Zale. "Who's the father?" He slapped Craig on the back again. "You know anything about that, Warren?"

"You aren't funny, Zale," said Craig, but his voice wouldn't stay steady.

"No?" said Zale. "You are!" The boys grew silent. Zale reached out for another slap on the back, but Craig brushed his arm aside. Zale's eyes narrowed.

"Fight!" someone said. "Slug him, Johnny!" said one of the scrubs.

That was typical, Craig thought. Leave it to the rinky-dinks. Always side with whoever could do you the most good. It made him sad. If things were different, if Zale were leaning on someone else, Craig knew he might be doing the same thing. No guts. If you weren't tough, you had to look out for yourself that way, be a politician, get on the good side of Zale and the rest of the guys who were.

"Hey," said Waldo Frampton. "Come on, you guys. We got a game tomorrow night. We can't be fightin' and all between ourselves. Come on!"

"Let it go, Waldo," said Eagle Duvall. "Let's see what Michelonis here can do on his own."

The circle of Owls pressed in around them. Zale put a hand on Craig's chest and pushed, hard. Craig fell back into Daugherty and was shoved back toward Zale. The stocky running back slapped Craig with his open left hand, then followed with a contemptuous slapping right. Craig stuck out his left hand for protection and felt a stinging sensation along his entire arm as Zale walked into it. Zale blinked in surprise, and his face darkened with anger.

A voice in Craig's head, the same one he'd heard when he'd broken into the clear momentarily against Allenville, said, "Now you're *really* going to get it!"

Zale lunged furiously to the attack, throwing punches in swift combinations, most of them landing on Craig's arms and shoulders. One of them snuck in over the lanky quarterback's outstretched left arm and popped him high on the cheek. "Attaboy, Johnny!" someone said. "Kill him!" said someone else.

Craig stumbled back against the crowd, slipped to one knee. Then something began to happen in his head. He realized Zale had hit him with his best punch. It stung in the cold. But it was nothing like the hit Eagle had landed on him on that first scrimmage play when he began playing Michelonis. Nothing like that at all. It was only a little hurt, the kind that felt good in the crisp air when you walked home. Zale had done his worst. And Craig Warren was alive and well and getting up. He thought of all the insults, all Zale's wise remarks.

"You're a jerk, Zale," he said calmly. "And you'll always be a jerk. You don't believe in anything you don't understand, and there isn't much you *do* understand. You—"

But Zale, white-face with anger, slammed in. This time, though, Craig brought him up short with a hard jab to the nose. Zale stepped back, then lowered his head and rushed in again. And again Craig's long left arm shot straight between Zale's flailing punches and landed in the running back's face. "My arms are longer," Craig thought, and the obvious truth surprised him. "I can hit him and he can't hit me. And if he does hit me, he can't hurt me. Not really. Not like I always thought he could."

The crowd was noisier now, most of the players rooting Zale on, but a few voices beginning to be raised now for Craig. "All *right*, Warren," shouted Eagle Duvall.

Zale kept trying to get close, but every time he came in, he ran into a stiff jab. When he did land a punch, another came smashing in over his arm and shoulder. Johnny Zale was no coward, but he hadn't bargained for this. It was like fighting a stranger, someone he'd mistaken for Craig Warren in the cold and dark, but this someone didn't seem to mind being hit at all. This someone could take it. And could dish it out.

"Kill him, Johnny!" yelled a scrub lineman.

Easy for him to say, thought Zale. It wasn't so easy to kill someone who wouldn't lie down and die, someone who didn't quit no matter what you hit him with. How did he finish a fight like that? What if he had to stay here all night?

Craig landed another punch, and Johnny Zale slipped on the damp grass and went down. He got to one knee, eyeing his opponent warily now.

"All right, that's enough!" It was Muldoon and the other coaches. Muldoon looked at Johnny Zale. "Glad to see you're getting in the right frame of mind for Brackenridge, Johnny." He glowered at the circle of spectators. "And the rest of you guys, the ones who couldn't fight to keep warm? *You're* out here cheering them on? Giving advice?" He shook his head as if in amazement. "Now shake hands, you two, and forget it. I don't care who's right or wrong. I don't care what started it. It's over. Get it?"

Zale got it. He pushed himself up and offered his hand,

looking at the ground. Craig took the hand, gave it a quick squeeze. Muldoon was right. It was over. The players scattered for home, talking as they went. So Artsy-Craftsy Warren had stood up to Johnny Zale and survived. Held his own, you might say. You could even argue he'd won. Who would have believed that? It was crazier than Waldo Frampton the day he dumped Coach Muldoon.

And Muldoon watched them go. When the last Owl had disappeared into dark, he turned to Buckwalter and Dykstra. "Well, I'll be!" he said. Even in the wintry shadows, the two younger men could see that Muldoon was smiling broadly.

Again the old way home. For the thousandth time he walked across the broad lawn of the nursing home. No touch football this evening. The kids had all gone home to supper. He turned up the hill, passed the small, familiar houses, the tiny alleyways in between. A fine mist, rain or light snow, spun in the cones of light under the street-lamps at each corner. The shadow walking under the lights seemed strange to him, elongated somehow, like the shape in a funhouse mirror. This was his neighbor-hood, the place where he had been born and had lived his whole life. Tonight it all looked different, the row of shabby houses as foreign as cottages on a postcard from some country he'd only heard of.

When he reached the corner at the hilltop, someone stepped out of the shadows under the large maples. "Hey," Craig said. "What are you doing out on a night like this?"

"I live here, practically," Dale said. "Remember me? The girl-next-door? You may have seen the movies? I—" she peered at Craig's face as he moved into the circle of light under the lamppost. She reached out tentatively, touched the cheekbone with gentle fingers. "Does it hurt?"

Craig smiled, then winced. "Only when I move my face."

"Well, Warren," Dale said, "the more things change, the more they stay the same. You're still a bruiser."

They paused under the streetlight, looking at each other.

"So," Dale said, "can I carry your books? I knew even rockhead Muldoon couldn't keep you guys past breakfast."

They walked in silence then, passing the two-story frame houses, the lights in the windows, the smell of woodsmoke rising from someone's chimney. "I just wanted to tell you," Dale said, not looking at him, "that time I called you a jerk—in the hall, remember? I was wrong."

"No. You were right. Even Eagle said so."

Dale groaned. "Worse than I thought. If Duvall said I was right, I must have been *completely* insane. Frothing at the mouth. I should have been given a saliva test."

"You were right."

Dale glanced at him. "Craig, we kid a lot, you and I. But—I don't know quite how to say it—I really am proud of you."

For a second Craig was confused. How had she heard about the fight with Zale? But then she went on. "You were right about that Frost poem. And with Zale and Eagle Duvall and those other goons in there—I know it isn't easy for you. I mean, you have to live with those guys. But you did it. You said what you knew. It doesn't even matter that it was right."

Craig didn't know what to say to that, so he didn't say

anything. They came to Dale's front steps. "Well—" she said.

"Well—"

She leaned forward quickly, raised on her tiptoes, and brushed his bruised cheek with her lips. Then she was gone, hurrying up the stairs and on inside the house. The door closed behind her. Craig Warren stood, his hand resting against the swelling on his face, while the soft mix of rain and snow settled around him.

TWENTY-ONE

*T*iny Daugherty's prophesied snow had not arrived when the Owls trotted out onto the field to warm up. It was cold, though. You could see your breath make little shapes in the night air, and most of the offensive linemen were wearing thin gloves. A huge contingent had made the drive up Route 219 from Brackenridge, including an exuberant pep band clad in bright orange and blue. The Owls were lined up in rows in one end zone, being put through calisthenics by Clint Gold, when an enormous shout went up from the Brackenridge fans, and the blue-and-orange Bison came out onto the field. They circled the playing area once, then lined up and began their own warm-up drills.

Craig found himself looking past Gold to the far end of the field. There he was! Number 44 peeled off from the rest of the squad and, with his back to the Owls, began to lead the blue jerseys in exercises. Jumping jacks. One-two, one-two, one-two. And then around with the trunk. Down for push-ups, everybody up and clapping.

"Come on, Warren," snapped Coach Buckwalter. "You

with them or with us?" Craig flushed. He realized he had started exercising in time with Michelonis. "March to the same drummer as the rest of us," said Buckwalter over his shoulder as he walked away.

As the Owls broke into specialized groups to loosen up, Craig took every chance to watch Michelonis. He was surprised to see the All-State tailback wasn't the biggest back Brackenridge had. Some of them even looked a shade faster. Still, there was something about him, the way he carried himself. It reminded Craig of watching basketball teams warm up. He could always tell the starters. It wasn't because they were the tallest, or even that they had the wiry builds or large hands that often tipped off basketball talent. It was that they carried themselves the way Michelonis did—they were loose and relaxed but intense all at the same time. And they expected their shots to go in, all of them, as if they saw the ball turning in the net so clearly even before it left their fingers that when it didn't go in, you could almost tell they didn't believe it. That was how Michelonis was. Whether he was passing to a receiver turning up along a sideline or trying field goals from bad angles thirty yards out, he expected the ball to go where he wanted it, as if it were already *there* somehow, and all that remained for him to do was confirm with his arm or leg something that had already happened in his mind. Craig was lost in the show Michelonis was giving, and he was sorry when Muldoon pulled the Owls off the field and back into the locker room.

"No creampuffs," Muldoon said. "No rah-rah. No win it for good old Oiltown High or for the Gipper or for Muldoon's wife and kids." He was pacing the small space in the center of the locker room, the Owls pressing in close. The air seemed dense, like before a big electrical storm. His cleats were loud on the cement.

A trainer stuck his head in the door. "Five minutes, Coach."

Muldoon waved a hand. The trainer disappeared and the door closed out the crowd noise, the bands. "No," said Muldoon, "this is for yourselves. Tonight is for yourselves. You grow up in this town and you wait maybe fifteen, sixteen years to be in this room, to be Owls. If you're lucky, you play maybe twenty nights like this. Then you're out, and most of you don't play football anymore. You come to the games, and there's the band, and the people cheer, and maybe a few remember you, but it's over. What you have to remember is what you did on a few nights like this one. A football game doesn't last very long. *Football* doesn't last very long. Out of every game, the ball's actually in play maybe seven or eight minutes. The rest is huddles and lining up."

The Owls were pressing in. Craig looked around. A few of them had their eyes closed. Johnny Zale's lips were moving as if he were praying. Even Eagle Duvall was carefully working a big fist into his open palm.

Muldoon took off the glasses. "You're a good team," he said, "maybe the best I ever had. You have that seven or eight minutes to be everything you *can* be. Don't come back in here when it's over with anything you saved up, any little piece of courage or effort you didn't give." He paused and looked around at the circle. "Well," he said, very quietly, "let's go see who's the number one team in this state." And then they were out, running through long lines of students toward the gleaming, lime-colored grass.

Captain Michelonis raised his arm, the whistle trilled, and he moved forward under the rattle of drums. The ball rose in the dark sky and the Brackenridge fans matched the Owl rooters in a long roar of approval. Johnny Zale gathered the ball in two steps deep in his own end zone, never hesitated, and came charging upfield. The white and blue lines came together violently, and a seam opened up in the middle of the Bison kickoff unit. Zale shot into the gap, but just as he was accelerating, a slim blue figure dove off a block and chopped him down. The blue-and-orange side of the stadium went crazy.

"Mike—Mike—Mike," they chanted. The public-address announcer's metallic voice echoed across the field. "Michelonis's kickoff returned by number twenty-two, Zale, to the Owl seventeen. Tackle by Michelonis."

Craig never took his eyes off number 44. He was all over the field, playing with a strange, intense joy. When the Owls assigned to go downfield and block him tried to carry out their assignments, they found Michelonis was never quite where they thought he was going to be when they started their blocks. He seemed to turn easily with them, help them in the direction they wanted to go, then send them spinning past harmlessly. It was like blocking long grass or water.

Gold found Duvall over the middle and shot a perfect pass between the Brackenridge linebackers. Michelonis sailed over Eagle's shoulder at the last possible second and batted the ball away. Zale swept the left end, sidestepping an onrushing cornerback, but Michelonis reacted quickly and slammed the Owl back out of bounds after a pickup of only four or five yards. He did everything —knocked down passes, made tackles, warned teammates of what to look for as if he had a direct phone line to the Owl huddle. When he tackled you, he gave you a hand up, and when a teammate missed a ballcarrier, he was there with a slap on the back, some quick encouragement. Craig remembered what Mr. Bryant, the Oiltown basketball coach, said about exceptional basketball players: "A good player makes his teammates look good! A great player makes them look *great!*" Michelonis was like that. Without him, Craig thought, the Bison were just another team, probably not as good as Oldfield or Fort Steel.

And the Owls were taking advantage of some of the weak spots, were making first downs, moving slowly but steadily into Brackenridge territory. Muldoon had seen it in the films. One of the Bison tackles didn't play low enough on defense—"He's a Kleenex tackle! Pops up!" Dykstra had said—and that was like giving Eagle Duvall a license to steal. When the Owls needed three or four yards, they slanted Zale or DeSales into the tackle hole and Duvall was driving the big blue tackle into the rest of the Brackenridge linemen. It was almost like turning him into a door and slamming it on the pursuit.

They had a second and six just inside the Brackenridge 30 yard line. Once again Gold tired the weak tackle, sent DeSales blasting into the line, and Duvall had his man driven well out of the play. It looked like a sure first down, but Michelonis had gambled, came shooting up from his safety spot even before the ball was snapped to meet DeSales at the line of scrimmage and cut him down quickly with a textbook tackle. DeSales got up slowly, went back to the huddle with a decided limp.

"Is DeSales okay?" Buckwalter asked.

"He'll be fine," said Muldoon.

That left the Owls with four big yards for a first down. Muldoon sent in a play. Gold dropped back to pass, the protection perfect. Willie White shot down the field five yards, then cut sharply to the sideline, looking back for the ball. Gold pumped his arm through, and the Brackenridge cornerback, trying to save the first down, took the sharp angle for the interception. He was going in the wrong direction when White planted his inside foot and cut back upfield along the sideline. "Chalk it!" shouted Dykstra as the speedy wide receiver made his move. Gold let the ball go, a tight spiral for once, perfectly on target. Even before the pass arrived, you could see Willie White had this one.

Then a blue blur flashed in front of the Owl receiver and was gone. The Brackenridge stands came to their feet. "Mike—Mike—Mike!" Duvall, White, and Krieg were out of the pursuit, off on pass routes taking them away from the speeding ballcarrier. Michelonis dashed along one sideline, and when the Owls hastily scrambled in that direction, he left most of them behind with a sudden cutback that took him across the field, picking up blockers as he went. "Mike—Mike—Mike!" Craig found his heart beating in time with the booming cheers from across the field. Only Clint Gold was left with a shot at Michelonis, and he made a good try. He hit the Bison tailback with a hard shoulder blow, tried to wrap his arms around the dancing legs, but it was as if the force of his own tackle moved his target out of reach. Like grass, like water, Michelonis went with the contact, relaxed, then burst ahead with a sudden surge of power. Gold was left sprawling on the grass, and Michelonis went in for the touchdown. A minute later he was quickly untying and tying his shoelace while the ball was landing well behind the goalposts for the extra point.

Muldoon stood with his hands on his hips, glaring at the scoreboard in disbelief. Then he turned to Dykstra. "How do you like that? We control the ball six minutes, don't let them touch it, call the perfect play, get perfect execution for once, and we're down, seven to nothing!" Muldoon sighed and pulled the baseball cap carefully down over one eye. "Things can only get better."

Brackenridge kicked off, Michelonis this time driving the ball through the end zone, and the Owls started at their own twenty. It was getting colder. Craig pulled the heavy black Owl cape close around his shoulders. He tucked his hands up inside his jersey, put them against his stomach gingerly to keep them warm. Oiltown was moving again, four and five yards at a crack. It was apparent, even to the Brackenridge stands, that the big white line was controlling the line of scrimmage, beating the Bison guards and tackles to the punch down after down. Zale hit for six, then for two more. DeSales made it a first down by lunging off-tackle for three big yards. Then it was Zale again for three, and once more for yet another first down. Muldoon watched grimly, tugging at his wiry hair, pacing back and forth along the sideline.

On first down Gold dropped back as if to pass, but slipped the ball to DeSales on a fullback draw. DeSales stumbled slightly as he tried to explode forward, and the ball slipped from his cold hands as the Bison linemen drove him to the ground. Players milled about, waving their arms like referees, each side claiming the ball.

"Everybody wants to referee," Muldoon growled. "Why don't some of them want to recover fumbles?"

There was a groan from the stands behind Craig Warren. Brackenridge had recovered, and the linesmen were moving the first-down sticks, pointing them toward the Owl end zone, which was only a little more than half the field away.

Brackenridge came out of the huddle with their wing-back to the right, the quarterback under the center. The ball was snapped through the quarterback's legs directly to Michelonis, and the tailback ran the basic Brackenridge off-tackle slant, the one Craig Warren had run a hundred times with the scout team. Eagle Duvall was throwing off blockers like a spaniel shaking off lake water, and he rose to meet Michelonis at the line of scrimmage, getting under the Brackenridge captain and throwing him back. Tiny Daugherty dove in just as Michelonis was going down and he and Duvall together drove the ballcarrier to the ground hard. Craig had an odd sense of living through something he had done before, but from a different angle. It was almost like seeing himself in a movie. He knew exactly what would happen before it happened, knew exactly how it was going to feel, but at the same time he was curiously apart from the action. *You owe it to them. Because you're the man. No one else. And this is your time.* Did Michelonis think those things? Craig wondered. Whose voice was it he had heard so clearly for ten minutes that Monday on the practice field?

But Michelonis had popped back up and was in the huddle, slapping his linemen on the shoulder pads, clapping, talking it up. He jammed down the blue helmet, wiped his hands on his thigh pads. Then he was back, slamming off-tackle to the other side, this time squirming and sliding his way almost to the Owl 30. *This is your season. They need you. To talk about. Dream of being.* Michelonis hit up the middle, was stopped, lunged forward one more time, picked up six yards.

The quarter ended then, and the teams moved to the far end of the field. Michelonis took it again, sweeping the right side for five more yards and a first down. Craig was breathing hard now. He felt as if he'd been running the ski slope for hours. The Brackenridge fullback slogged into the middle of the Owl line, and Pulaski stopped him, but not until he'd picked up three more yards. "Hold that line!" implored the Owl rooters. "Mike—Mike—Mike!" was the answering chant from across the field. And then Michelonis was running to his right, digging hard, and Duvall had him and Pulaski and still he wouldn't go down. "Reverse!" screamed Muldoon. "Reverse! reverse! reverse!" Michelonis had slipped the ball to his diminutive wingback, and the small Bison, hardly five and a half feet tall, Craig guessed, looking deformed in his outsized pads, was churning on his stumpy legs around the left end. Only Zale had a chance to catch him, and he knocked the ballcarrier sprawling just as he reached the flag at the coffin corner. The referee's arms shot in the air. Another Brackenridge touchdown! Michelonis was the calmest man in the place as his try for point was perfect. Brackenridge 14, Owls 0. Muldoon was livid. "We've got to play the defense we put on the chalkboard," he snapped. "We're running all over the place out there. Those weak-side defenders have got to stay home!"

"It's Michelonis," said Dykstra. "He's got us overcommitting on every play."

Brackenridge began to give up ground, but grudgingly. The Owls owned the line of scrimmage, but nobody could get past Michelonis and the other Bison defensive backs. It was slow work. DeSales was limping badly now, and Zale was taking most of the punishment. Gold's passes were not crisp, and he was obviously leery of throwing anything that might give Michelonis another chance to run in the open field. Twice they penetrated the Brackenridge 30 yard line, only to lose the ball on downs after a holding penalty the first time and a fumbled snap the second. When Brackenridge had the ball, they kept it on the ground, let Michelonis do the work. The Owls kept him in check most of the time, but it was like riding a stagecoach full of dynamite. Craig was so involved in the game, so absorbed in Michelonis's fluid moves, that he was startled when the gun sounded, ending the half.

TWENTY-TWO

The snow was falling slowly, soft as cotton candy in the beams of the stadium lights, as the Owls kicked off to open the second half. Gold kicked the ball clear out of the end zone—"One place Michelonis can't get it!" Muldoon growled—and the Bison started from their own 20. On first down Michelonis tried to sweep, but Eagle Duvall and Jim DeSales teamed up to haul him down. "Oh oh!" said Gene Dykstra. DeSales stayed down as Brackenridge huddled again. Muldoon and the trainer went out, but DeSales was on his feet even before they got to him, arguing with Muldoon about staying in. "I tell ya, Coach, it's nothin'!" Muldoon had heard it before. He waved to the bench and Waldo Frampton took De-Sales's place at linebacker. The home crowd stood and applauded DeSales as the disgruntled fullback hobbled to the sideline.

Brackenridge tried the wingback reverse that had worked so well in the first half, but Willie White refused to be suckered, kept the play from getting outside, and the wingback turned in to find Waldo Frampton waiting.

The play lost almost five yards. On third down Michelonis hit his end with a quick pass over the middle, but the rangy receiver juggled the ball and lost it as Johnny Zale plowed into him. Fourth down.

"Warren," Muldoon barked.

"Yessir?"

"Get in there at quarterback. Tell Gold to move to full. Let's see you move this bunch the way you moved that scout team all week!"

Craig was on the field almost before Michelonis's punt had rolled dead just across the Owl 40 yard line. This time there was no feeling of being in a dream. In fact, he had seldom felt more awake in his life. Everything—the falling snow, the lines on the field, the grim faces of the Owl linemen—seemed sharp and vivid.

"Number nineteen," shouted someone on the Brackenridge defensive unit.

"Watch the pass," Michelonis called to his cornerbacks.

That gave Craig an idea. He called the quarterback draw, hurried his team to the line of scrimmage, set both Krieg and Willie White to his left. The hole opened beautifully, and he shot through it, trying to run the way Michelonis did it, all out. He cut hard to his right, away from the Bison safety man, got a good block from Eagle Duvall, and turned on all his speed as he crossed midfield. The crowd was on its feet, its noise mingling with the wind rushing past the ear holes in his helmet. Michelonis had him in his sights, had taken the long angle across the field, was pinning him to the sideline. But Craig refused to go out of bounds. When the Bison safety hit him, he relaxed momentarily, then surged forward, pulling free and stumbling another five yards before one of the Brackenridge linebackers caught up with him and knocked him off his feet.

He was back in the huddle even before Paul Pulaski had raised his arms to gather the Owls into their tight circle. The ball was inside the Brackenridge 30. Craig called the option, hoping to spring Johnny Zale, but when he began his pitch, he saw that the defenders were keying on Zale, so he turned upfield and bulled forward, gaining momentum with every stride. When he came to Michelonis, he lowered his helmet and rammed into the All-State back with everything he had. The two went down together, and again the lights flared brightly when Craig rolled over to get up. Michelonis pulled him to his feet. "Way to run, nineteen!" Michelonis said. He was smiling, teeth white and even behind the mask. No doubt about it. Michelonis loved football, every bump, scrape and knock that went into it. "We have a first down," intoned the referee.

"Run a quarterback sneak," implored Waldo Frampton. Craig peeked at the Bison defenders, took in the size of the middle linebacker, and called a sprintout pass to the right. Nobody was open, so he pulled the ball down and ran again, making sure he squeezed every inch he could out of his forward thrust before the Bisons ganged up to drag him down. "Second and four," said the referee.

"Quarterback sneak!" said Waldo again. "Momentum, Craig! I got velocity, honest!"

Craig called the sneak. Pulaski and Mark Thomas got a good double-team block on the middle guard, and Frampton shot out from his guard slot, facemask almost clipping the grass, and chopped down the hefty Bison middle linebacker at the shins. Craig blasted through the hole and saw the end zone like a circle of light at the end of a long tunnel. He was going to be there. Nothing was going to stop him. And then the onrushing form of

Michelonis was in front of him like a face in a mirror. The hit jarred Craig to the bone, and he had just enough consciousness left as he went down to squeeze the football.

Someone was trying to pry the ball loose. He kept squeezing, drawing his knees up to protect the pigskin. "Come on, nineteen," said an authoritative voice. "Let's have the ball." It was the referee.

"Get up, Warren." Eagle Duvall was bending over him. "You can be hurt tomorrow. Right now, like it or not, you're okay."

He went back to the huddle. It was true, that voice he'd heard on the practice field. Was it only a week ago? It seemed like forever. The ball was spotted inside the one. All right. Time for Clint Gold. The Brackenridge line threw him back. Try it again, this time behind Eagle Duvall. Again, nothing. There? There isn't anybody there! The trouble with you, Gold, he almost said it out loud, is you think those tacklers are *there!* Quarterback sneak. Touchdown! Not exactly standing up, but six points all the same. Now Gold. Now the extra point. Good! And back upfield to kick off.

"Who do you want in for Warren on defense, Coach?" asked Buckwalter.

Muldoon was staring out through the slow-falling snow. "Bill," he said, "I got the most gawd-awful hunch. I don't know how it happened, or why, but that goofy Warren thinks he *is* Michelonis. And I'm gonna leave him out there until somebody wakes him up!"

Craig knew these plays. He had run them for a week, hundreds of times, had run them in his head thousands. Had dreamed them every night. And he knew Michelonis, felt close to him, a brother he never had.

191

Sweep coming. Craig rushed forward. Never a good tackler, but so what? What was tackling but wanting to? Hit. Hang on. A hand up. "Way to run, double-four!"

The fullback up the middle. Wait, wait. Yes, there it was, the buck-lateral. You could tell by the slight hesitation of the tailback. Come up hard, here he is! Whack! Hang on. All right!

Now. Look at that wingback. Something up over there. He's playing it *too* cool, too loose. Michelonis running right, but LOOK, the wingback slips his block and—PASS —and here's the ball if you can HANG ON and now RUN!

The Owls peeled back to block as Craig swung upfield, dropping a shoulder into one of the Brackenridge linemen and then coming up hard with a forearm to drive the potential tackler back and to the ground. Then he was off again, dancing past one defender, keeping his feet under him, using speed he didn't know he had to outleg another. They finally pushed him out of bounds at the Brackenridge 35.

Quarterback sweep right. Nothing there but if you SQUIRM and HIT and SPIN and now LUNGE for it. Five yards. Because they need you. *MIKE MIKE MIKE,* they were chanting, and not for you, but so what? Because it's all the same, Michelonis, and Warren and Waldo Frampton. You owe it to them.

Curl Duvall over the middle. And there's the ball, even before you throw it, so clear it's like a bright line in the air, and the arm comes through and IN THERE between the numbers and Michelonis knocks him down but FIRST DOWN.

Quarterback sneak. Come on, Frampton. Velocity. Move his mass out of there. Where is he? Come on, Mike.

Your season! And mine! All that talk about winning. What they want is to see us HIT. And NOT go down. Not yet. And not yet. YES. "Nice run, nineteen!" "Playin' the game, double-four!"

And who said that? Nobody out loud. Jam the helmet down. Make sure the hands are dry. No fumbles now. What matters is what it lets you do. How it lifts you up. Quarterback option. Tougher now. The hits harder. All of them coming at you. All that intensity, the energy. "First down!" Nothing like it, really!

Sideline pass to White. Michelonis there to bat it down. Now I see. You can't just look him off. Not *him*. Not Iron Mike. He feels things, knows what you're thinking. More than that. Feels your energy, senses the ball before it goes. SO! Think White. Throw him an imaginary pass, see the ball turning over in the lights. Make-believe it clear. And NOW pull it back and YES there's Krieg a step behind the corner and SEE it right where you need to have it, just like the backyard, the hands big as the hole in a tire, and THERE IT IS! Touchdown. Because it's not just for you.

Boot that point? No. Muldoon punches a cold fist toward the end zone. Go for two! All right. A fake to Gold off-tackle, put the ball on the hip, easy, easy, wait on it, go limp. And NOW there's Duvall slipping across the field, upstream against the flow of players, and NOW the arm whips through, and Duvall rises for the ball like a shark, the hands like immense jaws. Two points! We got 'em in our pockets, men! 15–14! Now go get 'em!

Clint Gold drove his foot through the ball, aiming it beyond the end zone, and it tumbled end over end high and deep through the swirling snow, dropping beyond the goal line, coming down six yards, eight yards deep where NOBODY would dare to run it out. Nobody.

Then Michelonis had it. And he was running.

Fourth quarter. The defense fired up, coming for you every down. *MIKE MIKE MIKE* beating like your heart somewhere a long ways off. This is your time. This is your season. But it's a long season and it tilts uphill like a ski slope every time you RUN and HIT and SPIN. A hand up. "Good hit," you say. "Good hit!" Tired like this, nothing hurts much. You can do everything, and there's always more time than you need. The body thinks for itself. The sneak. The option. Again the draw. Everything floating slow and soft, like the snow. Tough yards. *MIKE MIKE MIKE!*

Somehow there had to be a touchdown. Craig called the quick pass over the middle to Duvall, but Michelonis guessed right and had the wedge-shaped tight end blanketed. But still, there was time. There always was time. Craig backpedaled, looked to the outside, and there was Johnny Zale roaming out in the right flat as a safety valve. Craig zipped the ball out and the stocky receiver dipped and weaved along the sideline deep into Brackenridge territory.

Keep it going. Jam the helmet down. Dry the hands. Under the center, he looked the safety man in the eye. Was that a wink? Back to pass, the big defensive end slipping away from Daugherty this time and crashing hard. Duck under him, the bass drum booming deep in your chest, turn upfield and now DIVE for that first down marker. Got it! "Way to pick it, nineteen!"

The body a world to itself now, like the body of a racer at the end of a long one, running by itself long after the mind drifts off. Another option, turning inside the end, shaking off a linebacker, limp like water, like grass, then plunging on into *MIKE MIKE MIKE*.

It was beautiful, the snow, falling out of the black roof of sky. It was beginning to stick along the sidelines. The minutes were passing, and still there was something the Owls had to do. One more thing. And then one more. A play at a time. Where was that goal line? Was it under the snow? Maybe they passed it a long time ago, only nobody knew. They could drive like this forever, the other school chanting *MIKE MIKE MIKE*. All the special defenses. Another sprintout, taking no chances now, tucking the ball in and remember they NEED you to be MIKE and to KEEP running somehow, KEEP going and not DOWN. "First and goal," said the referee. He blasted his whistle, waved his arms. "Time out, WHITE."

Then Craig was standing in the huddle, looking up at the slow, heavy white flakes coming down out of the dark, looking *through* them really, to the tiers of seats rising like shadowy stairs beyond the beams of the stadium lights. They were up there. The little kids, the grade-schoolers with their khaki fathers. Joe Hugo. He was there. Funny Phelps and Quick Keller. Dude Perenchio. They were up there all right, the future and the past, what was and what was going to be. But he was now, and they depended on him. Something to dream. Something to remember. And beyond the shadows the scoreboard, bright as a Christmas tree, reading 45 seconds, reading VISITORS 21, OWLS 15. And he didn't know anymore if he was Craig Warren or Mike Michelonis. Didn't know if he was Coach Muldoon or Waldo Frampton or Arthur Craft. This was his season. He knew that. And there was something they needed him to do.

Muldoon sent in the play. It was a run or pass option, Craig Warren carrying the ball.

He scrambled to his right, carrying the ball at his ear, watching the Bison defenders scramble to cover the receivers, blanketing Duvall, White, Krieg. Gold chopped down one of the linebackers and there was the barest sliver of open alley leading to the end zone. He pulled the ball down and dashed into it, everything on the line now, the kids and fathers in the dark, not knowing, more on the line than a game even, and Michelonis, tough and gritty as they came, released his coverage of Duvall and rose up like his shadow to meet him.

TWENTY-THREE

The snow had disappeared except for a ghostly patch or two high on the hills, a shadow of white in the darkness under a stand of evergreens. The sky was a fierce, defiant blue and against it a few tenacious leaves, stiff and brown, fluttered like winter birds in the black branches of the maple trees. The donkey pumps were pounding in the brisk air.

Craig Warren came stiffly down his front steps, squinting into the November brightness. On the sidewalk, he looked out across the valley to the opposite hills, taking in the rows of brown and gray and yellow houses with the smoke slowly curling up from them through the bare trees.

At the end of the street the kids were out, the undefeatable kids, in winter coats, wool caps pulled down over their ears, still playing touch football with an ancient and outsized ball. Saturday morning. Craig remembered how it was, the sky spread out like a blank scoreboard, time left to play: all day. He stopped, invisible, almost, as a grownup, to watch them.

"Hey, Red, I'm Clint Gold. G'wan out for a pass!"

"Naw. *You* go out. I allus gotta go out."

"That's cause I'm the quarterback. You gotta do what I say!"

"Clint Gold ain't the quarterback. He's FULLback, stupid!"

"He's the *starter* quarterback, and you gotta do what the starter quarterback says."

"Not anymore he ain't the starter quarterback. My dad says it's that new guy now. You know, that Greg Warren?"

"Your dad doesn't know!"

"He scored two touchdowns, that Warren guy, and he passed one, too! He's real good. My dad says—"

The game swirled away from him then, the kids bunching and scattering across the yellowed, muddy lawn to a rhythm of their own, the rules and sides changeable as weather.

Greg Warren. He grinned ruefully.

He walked on down the hill, feeling good. Today, this November morning, he loved Oiltown. Across the street was the filling station and grocery store with the long coolers of Coke and Pepsi. And here the little print shop with the presses rattling away inside. He stepped around a small blond girl in pigtails, maybe seven years old, who was lost in a determined shuffling dance of her own. "One two THREE four, Who are WE for?" she sang to herself, flapping her thin arms.

Then he was passing the big stone houses, museums almost, that had been built a hundred years before by men who struck it rich when the oil was first discovered in the valley. The mansions were shabby now, mostly broken into apartment units, homes for church groups, run-down law offices. The big oilmen were gone, but their names were still the names of every east-west-running street in town.

Then the bridge, the creek snow-swollen and high, frothing around the pilings. And Main Street. The five-and-dimes, the picture show, McHenry's Drugs, the Army-Navy Surplus, the filling stations alternating corners, two Kendalls, a Gulf, a Penzoil.

"Hey, Warren! *Warren!*"

There they were, the downtown quarterbacks. Craig knew most of them by sight. Joe Hugo. Funny Phelps was the bald one with the red fringe of hair and the stumpy cigar. Quick Keller had the hard set to his jaw. Dude Perenchio, the one who looked like he could still play, his letter-jacket almost new.

"Warren, c'mere!"

Craig wandered over.

"Good game last night, kid! You ran real good!"

"Thanks, Mr. Hugo."

Hugo waved a hand. "Joe," he said. "Just Joe. Joey H to some."

"Loved that last TD," said Funny Phelps around the stump of his cigar. "You just flat run over that Michelonis, belly button to belly button! Just flat run *over* him!"

"What I want to know," said Quick Keller, "is what old man Muldoon had to say in the locker room to the poor sucker who let Michelonis waltz right through to block the point after."

"He wasn't too bad," said Craig. "Coach said it looked like Michelonis just made a great play was all."

"Some things," said Joe Hugo, "they just want to happen so bad, they're *gonna* happen. That game *wanted* to end in a tie!"

"Michelonis sure wanted to block that kick," said

Perenchio. "Looked like they didn't anybody even *see* him! And then didn't he get up in the air!"

"Just bad blocking is what it is," said Keller. "Believe me, if I was coach, *some*body'd be playing without a helmet for the rest of the week!"

"Ah, Quick, Quick," said Joe Hugo. "You saw a great play, a miracle almost. Don't spoil it. That Michelonis kid plays so good . . ." His voice trailed off.

Keller made a resigned gesture. "Ah, I know. It's just we coulda been number one, you know? We had it. We *shoulda* been number one!"

Hugo brightened. "Still three games to go," he said. "We'll make it yet. Hey kid. You starting at quarter against Sharpsville?"

"Don't know," said Craig, edging away down the sidewalk. "Coach didn't say anything."

"Muldoon's no dummy. He can tell a quarterback from a shotputter. You'll start."

Craig nodded, not knowing what to say, turned on down the street. The few cars passing through on 219 were stopped at the light, engines idling.

"Good game, kid!" or maybe it was "Good luck!" Joe Hugo was too far away now to be heard clearly. Craig turned and waved, a kind of awkward gesture of thanks, of salute. Then he turned the corner and escaped.

Congress Street was quieter, only a few thin women and oil workers with the weekend to themselves gazing into dusty store windows. Starting quarterback. He imagined it was true, believed it was. No. He'd *make* it true. That was *his* formula. Imagine. Believe. Act.

He glanced at his watch. Right on time. Noon, Dale had said. The library was a squat red brick building with worn marble stairs. Dale Davis was inside doing some research for Mr. Craft's class. Come to think of it, Saul

Bellow was in there, too. And the rain king, Henderson. Craig Warren took a deep breath of the sharp November air, then charged up the marble stairs, two at a time.